The Sweet Taste of Murder

By CeeCee James

~Dedication~

To my precious family

Chapters

1

The mercury hovered a gnat's eyebrow below 96 degrees on this unseasonably warm May day. In the shade of a striped umbrella outside the Sweet Sandwiches Deli, Elise and Lavina split a plate of macaroons with their sweet tea.

"Come on. You know you've always wanted to." Lavina waggled long nails at Elise, her crazy red hair spilling around the silk bandana she wore to tame her curls. "Those tickets are just for the taking!"

The tickets she referred to were for two free passes aboard the Norwegian Cruise ship. Her sugar daddy had just given them to her. At least Elise called him sugar daddy, but Lavina would call him her long-term boyfriend—who happened to be twenty-six years older than her own thirty-four years.

"Age doesn't matter," Lavina always told her. And, after seeing how happy Lavina was, Elise guessed she was probably right. Lavina was always sharing stories about cruises, Island hopping, and expensive gifts. But even with their expensive lifestyle, those two would always settle back like homing pigeons, watching Dancing With The Stars, over ice-cream.

Unlike Elise, who watched T.V. alone.

There was just one troubling thing. Elise had never met Lavina's boyfriend. She only knew him as Mr. G.

Today, Elise had barged into Sweet Sandwiches to search out her best friend. This shop was Lavina's baby, who'd purchased the business over three years ago. In a twisted irony, the high maintenance socialite liked deli meat, and was happy to don the rubber gloves and cut roast beef, sandwich-thin, whenever the customer ordered it.

Elise didn't have any room to talk about job choices. She was still searching for one after her husband of ten years left her for his secretary. Elise didn't know which part of Mark leaving was worse, that he left her in such a stereotypical way, or that he took the blender. Elise loved that thing and had been planning to use it for many more years to try and lose some weight.

Turns out separation was a much better alternative--over 195 pounds, and fifteen of that dropped off from her own body.

Still, after hearing how happy Lavina was with Mr. G on their last trip, Elise wouldn't mind seeing some of the weight return in the form of another man. But Elise wasn't holding her breath. It was time to get back on her two feet and figure out what the rest of her thirties was going to look like.

"Come on. You have to go!" Lavina cackled and continued to wave the cruise pamphlet. "Mr. G is busy that week, and I'd rather die than go by myself! I need my wingman!" She grabbed Elise's arm. "Please, please, please, please."

Elise stared at her nails. "When was the last time you had your nails done?" Lavina's manicure was perfect as usual, but Elise liked to yank her chain.

Lavina frowned as she looked at them. "Last week. Why? You think they're grown out already?"

Elise swatted at a fly trying to do the Cupid Shuffle on one of the cookies. "Just kidding you. They're perfect, just like everything else about you. Anyway, I've gotta get going." She watched the fly buzz away, squinting up at the cerulean blue sky.

"Where are you off too?"

"My first job back in town. Dog walking."

Lavina raised her eyebrows. "You know what people are going to say. Oh, how the mighty have fallen. They still have their nose out of joint since you left Angel Lake for that lawyer."

"Let them say it." Elise shrugged, pushing her dark hair off her shoulders. She had left Tennessee all starry eyed after falling for a big city lawyer who'd just happen to be eating in the restaurant she worked at. She'd let

Mark sweep her off her feet and into New Hampshire for the last ten years.

People had called her a trophy wife since he was eight years her senior. And it turned out to be too true. Brought out on special occasions, but otherwise, she had been left alone in their four-story Victorian built house.

She remembered clearly the day she'd read the text message. Mark's phone had been sitting out on the kitchen counter as he poured himself a drink. It buzzed, and Elise couldn't help but look at it.

Her name was Stephanie.

Elise had sunk onto the Victorian couch, one she never wanted, forced into her life along with a suffocation of silks and gaudy baubles, and pressed her fingers to her forehead. So overwhelmed. Scared. Angry. Betrayed.

She looked at her left hand now, smooth and white, showing a fresh indentation on the third finger. Softly, she rubbed at it before standing. "Let them say it," she repeated. Then, hugging her friend and getting a blast of the scent of hairspray, she continued. "As long as I have you, Vi, I'm good."

"Oh you have me," Lavina retorted with a chuckle. "I suppose along with a few canine friends, I guess."

* * *

At the grocery store, Elise scanned the cereal shelf. Ever since she'd been married, Mark had kept them on a strict food diet. Steel-cut oats for the morning, followed by a green smoothie.

Her eyes lit up when she saw the familiar red box with the leprechaun. Why not. I do what I want to do. She grabbed the box and turned it over. Her elation plummeted at the ingredient list. Over eighteen grams of sugar.

Don't care... so worth it.

"Wow, Elise... didn't think I'd be seeing you around here."

Elise looked up, startled at the unexpected voice. A tall man in dark police gear strolled up to her.

"Oh, my."

Brad Carter. The last time she'd seen him he'd been hitching his belt tighter around pants that threatened to fall off his skinny hips. She'd been leaving for college and waved out the window as the bus pulled from the curb.

"It's been a long time!" She injected a confident note in her voice.

Wait. What was still in her hands? The cereal? She casually set it back on the shelf and took a step in the direction of the Grape Nuts.

"You putting that back?" He grinned. "Seem to remember you always bringing a box to the camp-outs. You ate it around the fire like it was dessert."

"You still remember that?" Elise chuckled, and tucked her hair behind her ear. "Good memories. Sometimes makes me sad to be an adult now."

"So, you back for a while?" His tone was casual as he shook a chilled Starbucks coffee drink.

"Still drinking those, huh? I'm here for a bit."

"Like you already know, old habits die hard."

"You got me there. Wow, Detective huh? You've definitely made a few changes."

He looked down at his badge, his bicep flexing under his shirt. "A few changes huh? Don't tell me you still remember me as a pimply faced skinny teenager. Damn, has it been that long?" He looked at her, and his eyes narrowed. "It has been that long. Look at you." A slow grin spread across his face.

She snorted. "I guess I was skinny and pimply faced back then too."

"Nah. You were beautiful. You've always been beautiful. Used to get me tongue-tied back in the day." He cleared his throat. "I'm sorry to hear about you and your husband."

Inwardly, Elise cringed. Apparently, the gossip mill was still alive and strong in Angel Lake. She nodded and put on a brave smile. "Better to find out now, I guess."

His eyes flicked towards hers. "He's a rotten scum-bag if you don't mind."

Elise couldn't help smiling at his response. "I've called him worse."

He rocked back and forth on his heels, then cleared his throat. "Well, I should be going. Enjoy your Lucky Charms. I won't tell anyone." He gave her a wink and headed down the aisle.

She shook her head. The reality of being back in her hometown just smacked her full in the face. Everyone must know about Mark. That he'd cheated. She closed her eyes and took a deep breath. "Time to put your big girl panties on," she muttered, then lunged for the Lucky Charms.

2

Elise's first stop that morning led her to Ms. Perkins' house, her old school teacher as well as the first person to hire her since she'd been back in town.

"Well, look at you, Elise. I swear I ain't seen you in a month of Sundays. I'm so glad you are back. How's your mama?" The white-haired woman beamed up at Elise from a height of nearly two feet shorter. Her wrinkled cheeks were tinged the same apple-pink of her checked shirt. Elise leaned down to give her a hug and breathed in deeply. She smelled faintly of baby powder.

"Glad to be back, Ms. Perkins. Mom and Dad are good and enjoying their retirement down in Florida."

"Please, dear. It must be at least twenty years since I was your third-grade teacher. You're all grown up now. Call me Rose."

Elise nodded even as her stomach shifted uncomfortably. What was it about calling people by their first name after years of only knowing them by their last? It felt so strange.

"Rose. Okay, then. I just want to thank you for this opportunity. Your dog is amazing." She bent down to scratch the neck of the Pekinese. "And thank you for the recommendation." She had two more dogs to walk thanks to her old school teacher.

"My pleasure, dear. Just a little something to hold you over until you get back on your feet. Or, who knows? Maybe the start of a new venture. And I know my pup just loves it! I haven't been able to walk him as much since my hip surgery."

Elise made what she hoped was the appropriate noise in response. The Pekinese, a sweet little boy named Horace, licked her hand. "Actually, I've always wanted to own my own kennel and groom shop. This is a good start."

"I always knew you could do anything you put your mind to, even as a little girl. I think the only thing that ever held you back with was caring what other people thought."

"Really?"

"Yes. You were such a cute little thing. It made me sad to watch you ease back and stand in the shadows as your friends led the way." Rose patted Elise's elbow, which was nearly as high as she could reach. "But we all change, dear. It's called growing up."

* * *

Outside house number two, Elise checked on the lead fastened to the newest dog's collar. The sweet Golden Retriever, whose retired mother named Frodo, looked up at her panting. "What are you laughing at?" she asked, with a half-smile. "You're such a happy boy."

Her other charge, a brindle pug, promptly twisted her leash around until it was caught in between her legs. She let out a high-pitched squeal and jumped, trying to untangle herself.

"You did this to yourself, Winnie," Elise murmured and bent over to free the leash.

She slid the loop over her hand before turning to Horace. He pushed against her legs impatiently. "My goodness, are you ready for a walk?" That was a key word and set all three dogs lunging forward. She grunted as she tripped. "Fine, then. Let's get out of here."

Rose's earlier comment skirted the edge of her thoughts. Was it true that she always stayed in the shadows? Had she always been afraid to take the first step, content to let other's lead?

Her life with Mark sure had been safe enough. At least, she thought it'd been.

The dogs scurried forward tails wagging with pleasure and tongues hanging out. Both of her arms remained outstretched as they pulled her down the sidewalk. "Boys! Girl! Hold your horses!" She attempted to whistle, but could barely pucker, her mouth so dry from the effort of keeping up.

In unity, the three noses began sniffing along the ground. The hair on Frodo's back spiked up while the little dogs emitted high-pitched whines of excitement. In the next instant, Elise's arms violently jerked across each other as the dogs split directions.

"I'm the boss!" she cried weakly.

A deep laughed rumbled, nearly at her ear. Mr. Henry, who once ran the town's only gas station years ago, appeared from behind the hedge he was trimming. "Looks like you have a handful." His white-whiskered face creased into a smile.

"Oh, you could say they are a little energetic."

He came around the hedge and the dogs swarmed him, sniffing his shoes eagerly.

"Winnie! Horace! Frodo!" Elise hollered, as she tried to skirt the old man.

Mr. Henry held out a hand for the dogs to inspect. It was soon covered in slobbery kisses.

"Yeah, I'd say they are a mite energetic." He chuckled as he wiped his hand on the front of his overalls.

"I'm so sorry. Here," she offered her shirtsleeve. "Wipe your hand on this."

"What? Do I look like I can't handle a little doggy slobber? It's fine. Friendly bunch." He patted the Pekinese on the head. "Such a beautiful day made even better by happy dogs."

Just then a squirrel made its appearance. All three dogs dove for it. The leashes twisted along both sides of Elise's legs, and she fell backwards, landing on her butt with a loud squeal.

Mr. Henry blinked. His cheeks quavered with an effort to hold back a laugh. "Are you alright?"

"I'm fine." Elise blew a hank of hair from her face.

"You just need to show them who's the leader." He took the leashes from her and wound them up. In moments, he had all three dogs sitting. Elise climbed to her feet.

"Now, don't you let them pull you. Keep them walking right here by your side. And if they do pull, you just make them sit and see you're the big cheese."

Elise took the leashes and wrapped them around her hand as he'd shown her. "Thanks for the help!"

"You got this. Enjoy the beautiful day." With a nod, he retrieved his pruners and turned his attention back to the hedge.

Elise could swear he was chuckling as she left.

Dignity bruised, she headed down the sidewalk again. "You guys are feeling a little pesky today, but I've got you this time." she muttered. The dogs walked next to her, tails wagging and ears alert. Feeling more in control, she steered them to the trail that hemmed in the town's park.

Ford Park. A smile crept across her face as she entered the shade of the trees. She'd always loved this trail when she was a kid. Just shy of two miles long, it encircled the man-made Angel Lake the town was named after. Many summer days had found her there with Lavina sunbathing out on the grass.

They were nearing the back side of the trail that ran behind the business district. Every now and then when the dogs got too rambunctious, she made them sit by her side before continuing.

A familiar rumble vibrated through the ground indicating a train was on its way. Through the trees, Elise could just catch a silvery glint of the railroad tracks that ran on top of the berm.

Horace stopped, and his entire body quivered. He turned his tan-colored head back toward her and whined.

"It's okay, buddy. It's just the train. I won't let anything happen to you." Elise scratched his ears. He stretched his neck and sniffed the air. His black nose flaps moved in and out.

The other two dogs began sniffing. In the distance, the train blasted its horn in staccato bursts ending in one long note. Elise looked over her shoulder, but it was still out of sight.

All three dogs whined now and twisted their leashes around her legs in an attempt to move in different directions.

The horn blasted again, closer now.

"Come on, pups." Obviously, they weren't happy about the train for some reason. Elise led them off the path and down towards the lake.

The grass was thick and cool here. She sat down and immediately Winnie scurried into her lap. Frodo paced beside her before trying to climb in too. "Frodo, you're not a lap dog." Elise tried to push the big dog away, but he collapsed on top of her folded legs.

Next to them, Horace stiffened. A low growl curled from his throat.

The hair prickled at the back of Elise's neck. She peered through the woods towards the tracks.

The train was closer now, its horn still blaring. Elise tried to recall any other time the train had done this.

Like a rifle shot, the screech of the train's brakes overpowered the sound of its horn. Sparks flew as the metallic scream ripped through the air. All three dogs howled in sympathy.

Elise tried to wrap her arms around the dogs and gather them close. "Shh, it's okay," she yelled, her voice drowned out by the train.

Through the trees, the engine flashed by. Then car after car, all carrying the same sickening screech.

"What the heck?" Elise scrambled to her feet. The dogs trembled at her movement.

Boom! Like a bomb going off, metal gnawed into metal and exploded into shards. Elise jerked as every muscle spasmed.

She froze for a moment before running towards the noise. The train inched onward until it finally came to a stop. Her temples throbbed as the blood drained from her face. Confused, she shook the fear from her head and continued forward.

What had it hit? What was going on?

An eerie stillness settled over the park as the noise of the brakes quieted. On cue, all three dogs began barking. She continued to run, nearly flying off the ground at some points with her arms outstretched as the dogs dragged her after them.

Up ahead, black smoke encircled the rear of the car dealership that butted up against the tracks. Silver flashes of metal lay scattered in the gouged earth before the train's engine.

She could just make out the back end of a car. A tire.

Her heart stuttered. Only the the back end. The front half was wedged well underneath the front the train.

A crowd had already gathered at the tracks, all of them quiet and uncertain of what to do. Elise ran up to one man and grabbed his arm. "Is anyone hurt?"

He hitched his thumbs under his suspenders. "No, I don't think anyone's hurtin'. I reckon that driver is long past feeling any sort of pain."

3

That afternoon time bent in a way that Elise had never experienced before. There was an initial interview with the police, who soon dismissed her when they discovered she'd not actually witnessed the accident. The discovery that the man in the car was Cameron McMahon, the owner of the car dealership he'd died in front of. The numb walk home, only to turn with surprise that the three dogs were still with her because she'd forgotten to take them home. And the final emotional collapse that night on Lavina's couch, while her friend clucked her tongue and plied her with a martini.

Today, Elise wanted to shake it off. There was nothing that could be done for the poor man, other than taking a hard look at the cause of the accident to prevent it from happening again.

She'd gotten up, dressed and was actually headed out determined to use her gym membership, when a pitiful meow stopped her in her tracks. She looked around the front yard. There it was again, by the magnolia tree with blooms like snowballs at the corner of the house. A tiny face peered out from the branches.

It was the orange cat who'd taken to hanging outside her house recently. She squatted on the porch steps with her hand outstretched and made a few kissy noises. He didn't take much cajoling to join her on the porch. "Hey there, little buddy. Where'd you come from?"

The orange tabby butted her hand before running the length of his back against her fingers. His purr was deep and rumbling, making her pause to listen to it. It had been a long time since she'd last heard a cat. Mark had hated them. Her eyebrows crumpled together at the feel of the knobs on his spine. "Poor baby, you're so skinny."

Still frowning, she stood up. The cat rubbed his cheek against her shin. Her lips flitted into a smile, and she headed back to the kitchen.

After gathering a few slices of lunch meat and a dish of water, she placed them outside in a spot of shade.

The cat sniffed the lunch meat and turned away.

"What's the matter, sweetheart? You don't like turkey?" Elise scratched his head again, before looking down at her Fitbit— a birthday present she'd given herself. "Okay, then. I'll be back in a while to check on you."

After a few steps down the sidewalk, she turned back. The cat had swatted at the meat, and it dangled from his front paw. "You just like to eat alone, I guess." She chuckled.

* * *

Elise walked up to the last treadmill unmanned at the Muscle Motivators tiny gym. She took a couple deep breaths to mentally pump up for the run.

Next to the machine was a stair climber. Elise recognized Mabel, a recently retired postal worker, who now was practically the gym's mascot with her twice-daily workouts.

"Hey, lady," Mabel greeted, after a quick smile.

"Hi, yourself. Geez, you're incredible, Mabel." Elise couldn't help but admire the toned older woman's endurance. "How the heck do you do it?"

"Well, I tell myself, what's the other option? Give up and get ready for the Yellow Gardens?"

"Yellow Gardens?" Elise started a light jog.

"Yeah, the retirement home that old people go to pee themselves."

"Wow. That's depressing."

"Exactly. No Yellow Gardens for me. Not while I still have breath and can be moving and keeping strong."

Elise punched the button to push the speed past her normal rate. If Mabel could do it, so could she.

"So. Can you even believe it?"

"About Cameron?" Elise figured it had to be about him. Nothing this big had hit the town in a long while.

"Yep. They ruled it suicide."

The vision of the black Mercedes smashed on tracks flashed through Elise's mind. To do that on purpose? "Really? That's just so sad."

Mabel rolled her eyes, her face dotted with perspiration. "Are you serious? Why on earth would that man commit suicide? He had more money than you could shake a stick at. Heck, half the businesses in town owed him in some way or another. And, even though he was married, he honestly thought he was God's gift to women. You think he'd really off himself and deprive us poor women of his presence?"

Elise shook her head. "You're terrible."

Mabel grunted as she adjusted the speed on the climber. Her skinny legs pumped the stairs up and down. Elise eyed Mabel's ropy muscle and glanced down at her own pale legs, flabby in comparison. She wondered if she'd ever truly be able to run a half-marathon, the one goal she'd had since she was seventeen. A goal that always seemed to get derailed when it closed in on race day.

How fast was she going? 4.5? Oh Lord, she was going to die. With almost a whimper, she increased the speed, feeling like it was her heart she was ratcheting up.

"You hear what they found on his desk?" Mabel puffed out.

Gasping, Elise answered, "No, what?"

"A suicide note. Said he was leaving everything to his daughter." Mabel took a swig from her water bottle, her legs never slowing down. "'Cept he doesn't have a daughter. No children that we know about anyway."

"Seriously? Well, like you said, how can anyone really be surprised?"

"Oh, I think you'll be surprised all right. It turns out to be someone you know quite well."

Elise brushed the sweat from her forehead. "Who?"

Mabel slowed her incline and pressed two fingers against her throat to take her pulse. Satisfied, she stabbed the speed button to a stop. Taking a deep breath, she said, "Does Lavina ring a bell?"

Elise gasped, feeling foolish as soon as the sound left her mouth. But how could she not? Her best friend? Cameron's daughter? "That can't be right. I don't believe it."

"Believe it, chickee. The note said he was sorry for all the wasted time and then confessed that he'd always loved Lenora."

Lenora. A name Elise hadn't heard for a very long time. She was Lavina's mom who'd died when Vi was only six. Panting, Elise continued on the treadmill, her thoughts muddled.

Mabel grabbed a towel hanging off the arm of another machine. She wiped down the handholds of the stair climber. “I’ll see you tomorrow then?”

Still shocked by Mabel’s revelation, Elise nodded. Mabel tossed the towel into a bin and headed across the room to the weights. The crew over there welcomed her with cheers as soon as she stepped on the matt.

Lavina was Cameron’s daughter? Elise tucked her chin down as she jogged. Why did Lenora never tell her? Thinking back to kindergarten, she remembered the day Lavina’s mother had been committed to the mental hospital. Two teachers had nervously gathered in a corner before calling Lavina over. Lavina had been so cute in her pink dress and pigtails. Miss Clementine had gathered Vi in her arms and there she’d sat for the rest of the day.

Later, Elise had asked her parents what had happened to Lavina’s mama that made Vi cry. Her dad frowned but her mom answered that Lavina’s mom was not well, and it was her head.

From that day on Lavina lived with her grandparents, just three doors down from her own home. Elise hadn’t known any better and thought to have her best friend closer was just the greatest thing.

And for the next year Lenora shuffled in and out of mental hospitals and recovery centers in a downward spiral, until her death the following spring.

Lavina never made mention of her father or tried to find him. She'd always acted as if he never existed.

And to think, this whole time her father lived in the same town. Did Cameron know? Did he secretly watch Lavina grow up, filling with pride as she won awards, track meets, and eventually became homecoming queen?

Elise frowned. As far as she could tell, Cameron had never treated Lavina any differently than any of the other kids. He'd always been aloof when the girls approached. She remembered how he scarcely made eye-contact, dressed in his high tailored suits, his dark hair slicked back, and holding a cane. A cane that would look pretentious with anyone else, but somehow he carried it off with an air of savoir faire.

Whatever happened to that cane—black with a brass bulldog on top?

Elise shook her head. Who worries about a cane at a time like this? Frowning, she slowed the speed on the treadmill. Why hadn't Lavina called her about this? Did she know? Last night, when she was sprawled out on Lavina's couch complaining about her trauma, was Lavina silently grieving? Or was she completely oblivious and about to get blindsided by the note?

A shiver ran down Elise's back, and she flipped the machine off. Her legs felt rubbery as she wiped the treadmill down. Quickly, she made her way to the locker room. As she went, her eyes caught sight of Mabel.

Mabel's eyebrows were waggling as she talked animatedly to the crew at the weights. The other two women stood next to her shaking their heads and watching intently. Elise caught the word "suicide," and could just imagine the story spreading like wildfire.

She needed to find Lavina.

4

Before the gym doors had a chance to close behind her, Elise grabbed her cell phone and scrolled to Lavina's number. She hurried to the car, propping the phone against her shoulder as she scrambled for her keys. With the car unlocked, she sank down into the driver's seat.

"Hello?" Lavina's sweet southern accent filled the phone.

Elise felt a wave of relief. "Lavina, where are you?"

"Home, darlin'. What's the matter?"

Elise took a deep breath with her head rolling back against the seat. "Have you heard about Cameron leaving a note?"

"No! So, it was a suicide. My goodness. I would never have expected it from him. What did the note say?"

Elise swallowed. "I need you to sit down for this, Lavina."

"What are you talking about? Don't be silly."

"I'm serious. Sit for a second. " She paused. Squeezed her eyes shut and, like ripping off a bandaid, blurted, "It's an apology to you. He says he was your dad."

Silence on the other end.

"Lavina! Are you there? Did you hear me?"

"I heard you." A whispery sigh trailed at the end of the last word.

Elise bit her lip. "Did you know?" Her hand trembled, and she gripped the phone tighter.

"Yes. I knew."

"About the note? Or that he said he was your dad?"

"I knew he was my father."

The air in the car seemed stifling, and Elise jammed the key in the ignition to roll down the window. The dinging bell filled the silence as she tried to digest her friend's words. "Why didn't you tell me?"

Another sigh, this one louder. "I only just found out myself a few months ago. Mama had never mentioned a peep about him to me. Honestly, Elise, I hardly knew what to think of it. And with everything going on between you and Mark, well, I didn't want to add to your burden."

"You could never add to it! I'm here for you! Blood sisters?"

Lavina softly chuckled. "I remember that. Sixth grade wasn't it? Two peas in a pod."

"Yeah, and I was too chicken to cut my finger. You had to do it for me." A ghost of a smile appeared at the memory. "You should know I'm always here for you. Especially for something like this."

"Truly, I just was trying to ignore it. Pretend I didn't know, and it would all go away. I didn't want a relationship with him anyway. Too little too late. I don't think I could ever forgive him for abandoning my mama."

"Oh, honey. I'm so sorry."

"It's just all so weird."

"How did you find out?"

"Oddly, it was his housekeeper who first let it slip."

"Are you serious? How did something like that just slip out?"

"She came into Sweet Sandwiches one day to pick up an order. I remember her staring at me with huge eyes and talking a mile a minute in Spanish."

"Since when do you speak Spanish?"

"I don't, but the guy who stocks my deli meat does. He was behind the counter refilling the fridge. He asked her a few questions, and the housekeeper chatted back to him even more urgently, still staring at me like she'd seen a ghost. It unnerved me, to be quite honest. I certainly didn't know how to respond, so I just gave her the sandwich order and said thank you." Lavina mumbled now, and Elise could hear crunching.

"Are you eating? How can you eat at a time like this?"

"It's macaroons. You know how I am about macaroons."

"That's called stress eating."

"Oh." There was a pause. "That explains the tub of ice-cream."

"For crying out loud, finish your story! I can't believe you didn't tell me any of this earlier."

"So the housekeeper left, and Dan turned to go too. I practically had to threaten to whack him with the cheddar wheel to get him to talk. He was reluctant, but he finally told me." More crunching.

"You're driving me crazy."

"Sorry, sorry. He said the housekeeper kept repeating that I looked just like him. Like Cameron. And I was the reason their household was in an uproar. His wife threatened to divorce him because Cameron was ready to publicly claim me. Not that I would have let him. I would have denied every single word that came out of that man's mouth."

Elise closed her eyes again, trying to mentally compare the appearances of Cameron and Lavina. "I don't get how you look just like him. You have red hair for one."

"Oh, honey... you do know it comes out of a box, right?"

"You're telling me you don't have natural red hair?"

"Normally, sandy blonde."

Elise raised her eyebrows. "Lavina Sue Marie, I don't believe you. You were red-headed as a child!"

A soft laugh came over the phone. "Strawberry-blonde. That was grandma's doing. Grandma always used to say I had the mousiest hair. 'But we can fix that, darlin'. Every woman needs to have a sparkle.' From as early as I can remember every Sunday night she rinsed my hair with vinegar and then sat me in front of cartoons covered with a mound of tomato sauce and a plastic bag."

"You're kidding me."

"No. I'm sorry, hun."

"I feel like my whole childhood was a lie."

"Well," she sighed. "I know the feeling."

Elise's chest squeezed in sympathy. "Lavina, it's going to be okay. So what made you believe her? Believe the housekeeper?"

"It just felt right, like the missing pieces I'd always been looking for had finally fallen together. I started studying him, his mannerisms, his interests. I could see our similarities."

"I don't know about that. Do you think it could have just been her suggestion that made you subliminally see things that weren't really there?"

"I might have shrugged it off too, but he called me about a week later. Told me that he'd come home to his housekeeper crying while she fixed dinner. She confessed to him she'd spilled the secret. He said he felt like he owed me an explanation and wanted to know if I'd like to talk."

"What did you say?"

"I was angry. I yelled at him, asking him how he could even look me in the face after abandoning me all my life. Abandoning my mama. He apologized, but I said it was too little too late. And, then I hung up." There was a small sob on the end of the phone. "I didn't realize how true those words really were. Because it really is too late. But, I'm not going to let myself care about it now."

5

The next day, Elise jogged up the stairs of Mrs. Campbell's porch and rang the bell. Rose didn't need her today—Horace was at the groomer's—but Mrs. Campbell's two busy dogs always demanded daily exercise.

"Oh, hello dear. Come in. Come in! You're in the nick time. I just finished a brand new painting." Mrs. Campbell backed away from the open doorway, her cheeks folding into a wrinkly, crepe paper smile. The soapy scent of White Linen floated in the air as she shut the door.

Frodo bounded down the hall. Not for the last time did Elise wonder what the heck a fragile elderly woman like Mrs. Campbell was doing with an energetic young golden retriever.

"Come here, boy." Elise scratched the dog's neck as Frodo smiled, tongue lolling out. "You ready for our walk? Huh, boy?"

Frodo scrunched down into a crouch. His tail wagged frantically like a yellow beach flag warning swimmers of rough waters. Elise winced as it thumped hard against Mrs. Campbell's thigh. The frail lady staggered a bit and threw out a bony hand to catch her balance against the wall.

"He's just so happy to see you," Mrs. Campbell wavered, her voice breathless.

"Calm down, Frodo," Elise admonished. "Sit." She pressed her hand against the dog's back end. Frodo obediently acquiesced.

"So, last week in class, we learned all about capturing the beauty of a flower. Come see what I did." Mrs. Campbell tottered down the hall at the last word, leaving Elise no choice but to follow. "We had our weekly craft night. Mr. Thompson was there." She held a hand up to her mouth in a conspiratorial whisper. "Personally, I think he just comes for the wine."

She led the way into the living room where an impressive canvas lay propped against the wall. A bee took up the entire canvas. "I call that... beelieve." Her face shone as she smiled proudly at her work.

"Oh, it's lovely!" Elise nodded. If she squinted, she could just make out a blotchy green heart-shape in the corner. "And that is...."

"The flower. It's a bee and a flower. To show the contrast between different ways we can soar. Because we all fly high in so many unique ways."

"Ooooh." Elise tried hard to keep her face from showing skepticism. "It's lovely. Truly, you did a great job capturing the green. Life. Beautiful." She flashed her a grin. "Well now, I should get going before it gets too hot out. Frodo doesn't mind it, but Winnie gets very droopy in the heat. He'll just drag her along. Where is Winnie anyway?"

At the mention of her name, the pug poked a dark face out from under a blanket where she'd buried herself. Elise clicked her tongue and softly snapped her fingers to call the dog over.

"If I could just have a moment, dear. What is it with this younger generation always being in a hurry?"

"Just need to fly off." Elise chuckled at her own joke. It quickly faded as Mrs. Campbell peered over the tops of her glasses with lips pressed together in firm librarian disapproval. "Sorry," she whispered, and began fussing with the zipper on her jacket.

"Well, bless your heart. What I wanted to tell you was what Mrs. Packer shared with us at our meeting. It was right after our first glass of wine. Mr. Thompson had two and didn't think we'd notice." Her voice trailed away as her wrinkles settled into a frown.

"What did Mrs. Packer say?" Elise prompted.

"Oh." Reanimated again, she smiled. "Why, the most interesting thing crossed her desk yesterday. She was with her son—you know that nice, young police officer with the dark hair?— when he received a fax. It was the toxicology report from the coroner's office. Apparently, Cameron was poisoned."

Elise's mouth dropped open before she quickly recovered. "Did it say what kind of poison?"

"It said a chemical compound causing organ failure and heart attack. I wonder, isn't that something rat poison could do? Because I think it's awfully peculiar that there was an exterminator at the Wiggles Convenience store across the street just the day before. Tea, dear?"

Elise sank into a chair and accepted the delicate teacup Mrs. Campbell offered.

"Would you like a cookie to go with that?"

She shook her head in the negative. "How do you know the exterminator was there?"

"I heard it from Cecily—she owns the sewing machine repair shop, don't you know. They were there for years before Cameron's car dealership moved in. Quite ruined the neighborhood, she always said."

Elise felt a bubble of impatience rising in her chest and had to gulp at her tea to cover. Frodo bumped her arm with her head, impatient for his walk. "The exterminator?" she prompted.

"Oh, yes. Apparently, they'd been clearing their back lots. Rats everywhere. Cecily said she'd even seen one bobbing around in their pool!" Mrs. Campbell shivered. "Horrid creatures."

Elise placed the cup on its saucer. "What was the name of the company?"

"Oh, what was the name? Cecily told me." Her forehead rumpled. "Well, I can't hardly remember, dear. More tea?"

Elise bit the inside of her cheek, her thoughts spinning. "No, I really should go but thank you again for the tea. Come on, Winnie!" She whistled and this time, the little Pug scurried out of the blanket towards her.

After unfolding the leashes from her pocket, Elise snapped them on Winnie and Frodo. In his excitement, the big dog twirled in a circle. His tail swept the delicate cup off the table with a clatter, making both women squeal.

"I should have watched him better. I'm so sorry." Elise stooped to pick up the broken pieces of fine white china.

"It's not your fault, dear. Frodo strikes again." The older woman's face was grim as she shook a knobby finger at the dog. "What am I going to do with you?"

The dog sat with his ears back and looked contrite. His tail thumped against the floor.

Elise cradled the fragile pieces of china in her hand.

"The trash bin is just around the corner," the elder woman directed. Elise moved to the kitchen to deposit the broken glass. Her eye caught a bright splash of blues and yellows on the dining room table where a large vase of flowers sat.

"Those flowers are lovely, Mrs. Campbell," she said as she returned to the living room.

Mrs. Campbell's eyes brightened with pride. "Thank you, dear. Just clippings from my yard. Little did I know that I'd discover I have a green thumb in my seventies." She ruffled her hand through Frodo's coat and said, "Now, off you go and be good for Elise, you two!"

Frodo led Elise down the hall, with Winnie dragging behind. "One of you sure is ready for a walk." She laughed and began winding the leashes around her hand in preparation. "I'll see you later, Mrs Campbell."

Elise exited the house with the dogs and skipped down the steps. Frodo strained at the leash when he spotted a small creature scurry under the neighbor's hedge. Small and black. The dog tugged her over to investigate.

The squirrel skittered up a nearby tree with furious chittering.

"He's not your arch enemy, ol' boy. Now, let's go." She clucked her tongue at Winnie and looked at her Fitbit. Seven thousand steps. With a groan, she started into a light jog. Frodo and Winnie trotted next to her, tails wagging happily.

Elise took in deep breaths to maximize her oxygen. Her brain was spinning as her sneakers slapped against the sidewalk to the beat of the questions she had. Who had poisoned Cameron? Will they strike again?

6

It was noon on Sunday, and Elise was already late. With growing anxiety, she found one of the last parking spots available in front of the cemetery and nosed her car in.

And, it was sprinkling. Perfect. Why did it always rain for a funeral? Elise looked out the windshield at the sea of black umbrellas undulating around the grave site. Did she bring her umbrella? She glanced in the back seat. Her red one. She rolled her eyes at the thought of how she would stick out like a sore thumb.

Nothing to be done about that. She reached for the umbrella, fingertips just brushing it as it slid from the seat to the floor. After a grunt and a lunge, she procured it and climbed out of the car.

Elise snapped it open and scanned the funeral area. The seats were filled with people. She was surprised to see how many people she still recognized.

"Elise! Over here!"

A high voice grabbed her attention. Lavina waved from beneath her own bright paisley umbrella. Elise scooted into the empty seat, grateful for her friend. "How are you? Are you okay?"

"You know me. I'm always okay." Lavina's lips, covered in her signature red lipstick, broadened into a big smile.

Glancing around, Elise counted seven hats and three veils from where she sat. People still wore veils to funerals these days?

She located the blonde head of Mrs. McMahon sitting in the front row, hemmed in on both sides by men wearing dark overcoats. Mrs. McMahon dabbed at her eyes with a handkerchief as one of the men laid his arm across her shoulders.

It was the only sign of grief she saw. Despite everyone being there ostensibly to mourn the deceased man, the atmosphere was anything but somber. People chatted and smiled. Laughter broke out in the far corner but was quickly stifled by a clucking tongue. Apparently, some things were still deemed inappropriate for a funeral, even for one as disliked as Cameron was.

And then unexpectedly, a wave of quiet rolled over the crowd and quickly dissolved into furious whispering. Elise spun around to see what caused the ruckus.

A wheelchair bumped up the aisle. Seated in the chair was a tall, skinny man, his face drawn and solemn. He seemingly did not notice the disruption he caused the crowd of mourners. Bereft of an umbrella, he huddled under a plaid blanket that covered his legs.

The young woman who pushed him appeared to be in her early twenties. At first glance, her clothing seemed well put together, but under closer scrutiny, Elise noticed the frayed edges of her black jacket and scuff marks on her shoes. Her pale wrists seemed too dainty to wield the big man in the wheelchair. And almost to prove the point, the wheels stuck fast on a knob of grass. She heaved, her arms trembling, and finally made it over. The man's head bobbed at each bump as she struggled to push him through.

Elise tried to see her face, but the woman's features were hidden by a black fedora.

The whispering abated the farther he came up the aisle. The young woman glanced ahead and nudged a pair of glasses higher on her nose. She located a place for the two of them and determinedly shoved the wheelchair towards it.

With a few more bumps, the young woman got him to the front. After putting the brakes on, she settled next to him in an empty chair. She fussed over the blanket, making sure he was covered, and then opened an umbrella and held it over them both. She took a deep breath before crossing her legs daintily at the ankles.

Around them, the swell of conversation grew. Elise could just make out a few words. "Is that him?"

"Yep, that's him."

"Probably come to spit on the grave."

Elise studied the man further. Hunched in a tweed overcoat that lay in deep wrinkles around his waist, the man stared straight ahead. He looked to be in his late fifties. Elise wondered at the relationship between the young woman and the man. His injury did not seem recent as his legs held the thin boniness of someone trapped in the chair for a very long time.

His eyes remained hidden behind black-framed glasses, his face frozen in an unreadable expression. His hands lay limply folded in his lap. Suddenly, he ducked his head to whisper to the young woman. She looked toward the front and nodded in return. His face broke out into a grin, and he let out a low chuckle. The young woman's lips flickered in a small show of amusement as she returned her attention to the front.

Elise nudged Lavina. "Who is he?"

"Oh, honey. You've missed out on so much in the ten years you've been gone. How can you ever expect me to get you caught up on all the gossip?" Lavina plucked at a small piece of lint caught on the front of her hot pink sweater. Never one to shy from color, even at a funeral, Lavina flicked the lint before patting her brilliant red hair piled high in curls up on her head. "That is Mr. Davis. He's been in a lawsuit with Cameron for nearly as long as you've been gone. It's just been dragging out in court."

"Who's the woman?"

Lavina flashed a quick gaze over to study her. "I've never seen her before. Perhaps his assistant?"

"Well, what happened? You going to tell me?"

"Mr. Davis used to work with Cameron years and years ago, back when Cameron was also a young man. I saw a picture of them in the newspaper advertising a butchering business they'd started together. Cute young man, both in their early twenties. They're always so delicious at that age." Lavina sighed and licked her lips at the memory.

"Lavina, focus!"

"Oh, pooh. You never want to hear the good stuff. Anyway, Mr. Davis showed back up in town about ten years ago and reunited with Cameron. It did not go well. I believe there was some squabble over money that left our dear Mr. Davis quite upset. There were threats made and a screaming match. I heard it was quite spectacular. Then Mr. Davis drove off the car lot with his teenage son sitting in the front seat with him. From there they just disappeared." Lavina's eyes widened dramatically. "No one heard from Mr. Davis for days and a missing person's report was filed."

"And?"

"Turn's out a local farmer caught sight of his car at the bottom of Reicher cliff." Lavina leaned close to whisper and a heady scent of Lily of the Valley rolled between them. "Poor man was pinned in his car with his son gone to be with the angels. Brake lines were just hanging by a thread."

Elise felt the blood drain from her face. "So... foul play then."

"The foulest. Or so a little bird told me. Our police department spent one lick of a minute investigating the accident before calling it a natural event. People didn't look so kindly at Cameron after that." She tipped her head in the "you know what I'm talking about" way.

"So, what about this lawsuit?"

"Mr. Davis has been after Cameron in a civil suit all this time. Apparently, he has proof that Cameron's hand was in the crime. Hidden away someplace safe, is how the rumor goes."

"What the heck? How could he have proof and the state not go after Cameron?"

"I don't know. This is the first time any of us has seen Mr. Davis's face in all these years."

"Where has he been all this time?"

"I've heard he's been staying at the Riverside Retreat and Wellness Center out in Tallahassee. They're the cutting edge in the treatment of nerve and brain damage." Lavina raised a plucked eyebrow.

Elise shot another look at Mr. Davis. As if he sensed her interest, he shifted in his chair until he could return the stare. The overcast sky flicked its reflection across the lenses of his glasses. His lip lifted in a sardonic grin, and he raised two fingers in a mock salute.

Elise couldn't believe his attention and gave a furtive glance over her shoulder to see if there was someone else he was looking at. No one appeared to have noticed. She glanced back. Mr. Davis continued to hold her gaze for a moment more before finally releasing it to face front. She exhaled deeply and unconsciously rubbed her throat.

Beside Elise, Lavina scrolled through her phone. "Big deal, huh?" She continued to drone away, oblivious of the interaction.

"Despite his thinness, he definitely doesn't look like a frail man."

Lavina shook her head before jamming her phone back in her purse. "Nobody said he was. I think he even had Cameron shook until his accident. Now would you check out all those planters?"

A row of silver planters filled with stalks of flowers lined the front like soldiers guarding the unknown tomb. Elise quickly counted. "Twenty-nine of them. So odd."

Then, touching Lavina's arm. "You sure you're okay? Have people talked to you?"

"I'm fine. You know my motto: never let them see you sweat."

Around them, people quieted again. A priest adorned in heavy vestments walked to the vestibule. He folded his hands and stared out at the gatherers. "Dearly beloved, today is a sad day," he began.

Lavina snorted next to her, before grabbing a hanky from inside her purse. She dabbed at her eyes. "A very, very sad day." She nodded. Despite her sarcasm, Elise saw some real tears.

7

After the funeral, Lavina looped her arm through Elise's. "Let's skip the reception. I really don't want to be interrogated by any old biddies wanting to know why my name was written on that note."

"You got it," Elise said. "How about a glass of wine instead? StarMart has a riesling on sale."

Her friend flashed a smile. "You read my mind."

They made quick work through the grocery store, procuring a few food items and the wine. At the last moment, Elise added a couple cans of cat food.

Lavina pushed the cart up to the checkout and began unloading it onto the conveyer belt. Beside them, an array of candy bars practically waved at them like happiness banners on a rack. Her stomach rumbled. She reached for one, feeling like a six-year-old kid about to sneak into the cookie jar. Her eyes caught sight of the purple Fitbit on her arm, and she groaned. "Don't want it all to be for nothing," she muttered.

"What, honey?" Lavina asked.

"Nothing. Just trying to be good is so hard."

Lavina arched an eyebrow. "That's what I always say." She smiled decadently.

"How are y'all doing this morning?" The older blonde cashier smiled at them as she scanned the first item with a beep. Her name tag said, "Home of excellent service, I'm Annie."

"Good." Both ladies nodded.

"Been such a strange week, don't you think? It's just so mysterious about poor Herman." Annie shook her head before scanning another item.

"Herman?" Elise lifted out the case of water bottles.

"Hun, you can just leave that right in your cart," Annie said. She waited expectantly until Elise returned it with a grunt.

"Oh my goodness." Lavina's eyes widened. "I totally forgot about the little guy."

"Poor thing's been missing since the day Cameron died. No one's seen hide nor hair of him." Annie ran the scanner over a can of green beans with no effect. Squinting, she peered through the bottom of her glasses at the bar code before slowly typing it in. The equipment at the StarMart was still from the 1980's.

"Who's Herman?" Elise whispered. Lavina turned to answer, but Annie butted in.

"You haven't heard of Herman? Girl, hush your mouth. Where you been, under a bush?"

"I just got back to town."

Annie frowned at her as if branding her a stranger. Then the lines on her face smoothed. "Oh, that's right. You're the one who married that lawyer fellow. So hoity-toity. How's that going?" Her eyes glinted. She knew full well how it was going.

Elise decided not to take the bait, instead, she set the riesling bottle on its side to roll down the belt. "It is what it is. Now, how about Herman? Was he a friend?"

"No." Annie snorted like Elise was a few walnuts short of a fruit cake. "He was Cameron's buddy. A little doxie. Went everywhere with that man. Even on car rides. Just sat in the passenger seat as happy as could be."

"Unless you got on his bad side," Lavina interjected.

"That's true. That little bugger could carry a grudge longer than my ex-mother-in-law, but he was the friendliest thing with Cameron and his wife. But you didn't want to cross him, or you were in danger of losing a finger."

"What a peach." Elise laughed.

Annie scanned the box popcorn before turning it over to look at the ingredients. "This ain't natural," she said before bagging it with a disapproving look on her face.

She scanned the toilet paper. "You know, we have the generic on sale right over there."

Elise shook her head slightly. "I'm okay."

"You're paying three times as much for this one." Annie shook the rolls to punctuate.

"It's okay. I like this brand." Elise replied.

"Hoity-toity bum to match your husband, I guess." Annie sniffed and discarded the toilet paper in the bag as if it were reprehensible.

Lavina shot a look at Elise and powered on. "So, back to Herman. He's missing?"

The distraction worked. The next few items were scanned with scarcely a look. "He disappeared the day Cameron died."

"Did he run away? Get lost?"

Annie shook her head. "Nope. His collar was left on the floor of the dealership." Her watery gray eyes widened. "Just the collar lying there all innocent like."

"So, you think someone took him?"

"Sure enough, someone did. He witnessed the crime."

Elise frowned. "How'd you hear that this was crime?"

Annie laughed. "Being married to a lawyer sure didn't smarten you up none. You tell me why a rich man like Cameron would kill himself? That man had more money than brains, and he warn't stupid. He had the entire town eating out of the palm of his hand." Annie lowered her voice to a dramatic whisper. "And that includes more than half the women."

Lavina rolled her eyes.

"It's true. And he'd let them. Except for one. Poor lady. The last few weeks of his life he treated her just as cold as ice."

"His wife?"

"No, he was always kind to her as far as I saw. I'm talking about his secretary. He treated her like she could drop dead there at his feet and he'd step right over her body."

"When did you first notice this?" Elise listened carefully.

"Probably two months ago. She was standing in that aisle right over there." The cashier indicated the back of the store with her thumb.

Elise turned her head. "Which one?"

"That one. Aisle eight. That's the feminine product aisle." Annie's voice lowered into a hushed whisper. "She was at the end where the pregnancy tests are."

"That ain't no news that Sylvia's pregnant." Lavina sniffed. "After all, she's married."

"She's married alright." Annie retorted sharply. "But that didn't stop her head turning when Cameron came around."

"You're saying she cheated on Frank? How on earth would you know this?" Lavina looked genuinely shocked.

Annie shrugged. "You hear things in a small town. Besides, I'd seen with my own eyes the two of them sneaking into his car one night. They went behind the storage units and were getting busy, if you know what I mean."

Elise frowned. "What were you doing behind the storage units?"

"I saw the nose of that black Mercedes as I was driving by and thought it might be stolen. Had to turn around and look."

"How do you know that baby isn't Frank's?"

"Rumor has it Frank ain't so good in the baby making department. Last I heard they were heading towards adoption." She smirked. "Doubt that's in the cards anymore. Probably more likely headed for divorce. That poor girl got dumped by both Cameron and her husband. Who knows what will happen now."

"Annie, that's just awful!" Lavina's face was red. "You're spreading rumors."

"These ain't rumors! He was firing blanks. Now, his wife is all swelled up with a baby. He knows! And, what makes it worse is that there's always been bad blood between those two men. I remember two years ago when they got into a squabble outside Ben's Bar and Grill. Seems to me that fight was real nasty."

"That was a crazy fight," Lavina interjected. "I remember Frank popped one off and hit Cameron straight in the mouth."

"He turned and ran before Cameron caught his balance," Annie continued. "Frank was always more a chicken than a rooster. Well, having his wife pregnant probably fueled his courage. I sure think a positive pregnancy test sounds like a motive for murder to me."

8

Tuesday was setting up to be a good day. After endless nagging, Elise decided to finally take Lavina's advice and get a hair cut. She really did need something new to recognize the changes in her life, and was pleased they could see her right away.

Before she knew it, she was draped in a black plastic cloth and being led to the sink. Several older women sat under hair dryers, their hair pinned up in curls. Since returning to her hometown, Elise sometimes felt as if she'd taken a step back in time. As if the move could erase the ten years she'd been married.

If only it were that easy. She touched the dip in her wedding finger. The divorce was to be finalized in just two weeks. She knew she should feel happy but felt grief instead.

Shake it off. She smiled at the beautician. Carla was her name, a cute twenty-something gal with purple tips in her hair. Maybe not a total step back in time after all.

Just as she was being seated, the bell above the door rang.

"Sylvia?" a deep male voice called out.

"She ain't here, Frank. You leave her be!" One of the other beauticians yelled back.

Frank narrowed his eyes before yanking the door closed so hard the bells threatened to fall off.

"Well, there goes some bad news." Carla primly pressed her lips together. "I always knew he was up to no good."

Elise could barely hear with the water running over her head. She squirmed in the chair, wishing Carla would hurry up. Her neck ached against the sink.

Water sprayed across her face as the beautician momentarily lost control of the hose. "Carla!" Elise squinted up at her.

"I'm sorry, love." Carla leaned over her, giving Elise a whiff of some very stale floral perfume. She came back with a towel and patted the water off Elise's face.

The patting was worse than the spray. She could only imagine what her mascara looked like now.

"That's Frank, huh? I've never seen him before," Elise finally managed to say once the terry-cloth torture was over.

Carla helped her back up and followed her to the chair. "Yep, that's Frank. He's been nothing but trouble ever since he moved here."

"Why's that?"

"He came here after just getting released from jail. Nobody would hire him. So, he ended up moving to the west end of town and starting up some shady business."

"What was he arrested for?"

"He stole somebody's car."

Elise felt her eyebrows raise. A car thief who hated a car dealer. Seemed like a small world. "What does he do now for work?"

"He finally got Old Tom from the pest control place to hire him. Tom owns RatsOut."

Elise straightened in the chair, remembering the toxicology report.

Carla sniffed. "He's just darn lucky anyone was willing to hire him with his background." She reached for a comb from her drawer. Carefully, she began to draw it through Elise's hair. A snarl appeared, and Carla leaned for her conditioning spray, giving Elise another uncomfortable wash of perfume. "I'm surprised Cameron didn't have him run out of town a long time ago." She spritzed the bottled and continued with the comb.

Elise winced as Carla worked on a snarl. "Why do you say that?"

"They had some bad blood a while back. Actually got into a fight outside Ben's Bar and Grill. The rumor has it there was a gun, but by the time the cops got there, they'd both disappeared. And, of course, nobody seen nothing."

Like a magician, Carla whipped out some hair clips from her never-empty pockets. She pinned up Elise's hair and grabbed for her scissors.

"A fight?" Elise nodded her head a smidgeon. "I heard about this the other day."

"It was over quick. Sally was there." Carla yelled across the salon to the other beautician. "Hey, Sally? You remember that fight outside the bar and grill last year?"

Sally looked up with a gossip rag in her hand. Her bored expression lifted slightly, and she stood up from the stool behind the counter.

"How could I forget. Jacob was the one who broke them up."

"That's Sally's boyfriend," Carla whispered down at Elise. "He sure did, honey! He did real good. Do you remember anything about it?"

"Well, I was still inside, so I didn't hear much. But Jacob said that Frank was yelling about how he wasn't taking any more of that. And Cameron shoved him right in his face and said he'd see him tonight."

"Cameron hit him first?" Elise asked.

"I wouldn't say hit him, more like a steam shovel to the face. Just pushed him right over. Then Cameron went scrambling inside his jacket, and Jacob says he saw a gun. But by then all the bar was emptying so Frank just up and ran off."

“Was there a police report?” Slowly, her chair was being spun away from the mirror. Elise tried not to be anxious. It was just a trim. Surely it was going to be okay. Her gaze dropped to the floor where an alarming length of her hair had just fluttered down.

“What was there to report?” Sally shrugged. The phone rang, and she meandered back to her post.

“See, it was soon after that Frank got arrested for stealing a car. They sent him away for eight months. Then his ol' lady started to work for Cameron.”

“Cameron hired his enemy's wife? That doesn't make any sense. She worked with him the whole time?”

“First time she ever had a real job, as far as I know. Poor thing, I don't know what she's going to do now. No one understood why he hired her in the first place. It's like I told ya. Cameron was up to no good. Good riddance, I say, like the rest of the town. Fate has a funny way of fixing ya.”

“Everyone's been saying it wasn't a suicide.” Elise said.

“Suicide nothing. I heard he was foaming at his mouth, and his throat had claw marks.” Carla flicked her hand out in the air, her nails curled downward. “Just gives me the shivers, to think of dying like that.” She pulled the comb through Elise's hair again and made a few more careful snips.

"You sure know a lot about all of this."

"You just haven't known where to go for gossip. I've always got the good stuff. Ain't that true, Sally?" Her fingers flew through Elise's hair fluffing it up, as Sally yelled back an affirmative. "There. That looks so nice. Everything put back to right."

"Put back to right?"

"Yep. I cut the hair until it's just right. Like doing a math problem. Can't stop until it's perfect. Hair cutting has been the only thing to really help me with my OCD ways." Carla reached for the hair dryer and a round brush.

With the dryer going Elise settled back into her thoughts. So, if it was true Cameron was murdered, why was no one else talking about it?

Carla quickly spun the chair back to face the mirror.

"Honey, you like that? What do you think?"

Elise felt her eyes widen. Definitely not a trim. Cautiously she reached up to touch her newly layered cut, resting now just against her collarbones. Mark would've freaked if she'd ever cut her hair this short before.

"Shake it, honey. See how it feels."

Elise gave her head a slow shake. The hair moved and settled back into perfect waves. A smile crept across her face. "I love it."

9

Elise rounded the corner and jogged up the street lined with quaint houses and white picket fences. Gingerbread Lane, she'd called it as a kid, and had always wanted to live there. Quickly, she jogged past three brown houses and one brick to turn down her friend's driveway.

Lavina sat on the porch wearing a wide brimmed sunhat. She lifted a frosted glass of tea in greeting as Elise puffed up the stairs.

"Well, now. That's a cute little haircut. Finally decided to doll yourself up, I see." Lavina cast a critical eye at Elise's yoga pants. "But we must do something about your wardrobe choice."

Elise flipped her hair off her shoulder and shook it, relishing the cool breeze on the back of her neck. "I'll admit, I love it. And you leave my clothing alone."

"You look a bit hot, darlin'. You run all the way here? I don't know what's gotten into you with all this exercising business." Lavina wrinkled her nose. "Makes you all sweaty and stuff. Sweet tea?"

"How'd you know I was coming?" Elise collapsed onto the wooden steps with a sigh. Leaning back against the porch pillar, she eyed the extra glass as Lavina filled it from the pitcher.

"Oh, honey, I knew someone would be showing up, and I always like to be prepared." She passed the glass down to Elise. "If the goal was to get your new hairdo hot and sweaty, well sugar, there are better ways. Now, what else have you been up to today?"

"Just trying to get ready for that 5k next month. By the way, I heard some good gossip at the hair salon today. You know that guy, Frank? The one the grocery clerk was talking about? Works at the pest control?"

"Oh, sure. I know Frank. He used to work at the gas station. The last time I saw him, he gave me a wink like there was no tomorrow. He shone his flashlight in my face and offered to check under my hood." Lavina sniffed. "Of course, I told him where he could stick his teeny weenie Maglite."

"Lavina!" Elise laughed. "You are such a flirt."

Lavina puckered her lips for a fresh application of Auburn Red glossy lipstick. "Now, don't be jealous. It's not a good look for you."

"Jealous of what?"

"I've still got it. And, you are the one in definite need of a man." Lavina ran her fingers through her hair before scrunching up one of her red curls.

Elise rolled her eyes. "Anyway, according to the gossip, they think he might have killed Cameron."

"Couldn't have happened to a more deserving man."

"You are insufferable. The point is, do you think Frank knocked him off? Because we already have a half-a-dozen why's."

Lavina nodded. "A glorious man like that? Hard to believe." She counted reasons off on her fingers. "Scum bag. Cheat. Fraud. Misogynistic. Cheapskate. Abandoned his child. Correction, children."

"He may be all those things." Elise sighed. "Never mind, he was all those things. But did he deserve to be dumped like a mud slurping carp into a Mercedes to be hit by a train?"

Lavina arched one perfectly manicured eyebrow. "It does seem fitting."

"Speaking of fitting, Sylvia's going to have your sibling. You ever think about that?"

Lavina stared down at her with dark rimmed eyes. "Elise, I am far too old to get a sibling."

"But that's what's happening. It has nothing to do with age."

Lavina sighed and rested back into her chair. She tapped her long nails irritably on the table.

Elise took a sip of tea. The frosty sweetness rolled over her tongue with just a hint of lemon. "Mmm." She licked her lips appreciatively. "I'll have to admit, you sure know how to make sweet tea. Almost as good as Grandma Babe's."

"She still coming by your place?"

Grandma Babe was the owner of the small Mom and Pop restaurant down on Main Street, tucked in between an antique store and a cupcake shop. She made the best biscuits and gravy this side of the state line. She was also Elise's neighbor and convinced Elise was starving. Every Wednesday she came over with a plastic tote filled with the week's various leftover dishes that Elise dutifully filed in her freezer. For this Elise paid Grandma Babe a measly sum and gave her the satisfaction that the poor skinny neighbor girl would be fed for another week.

Win-win in Elise's eyes.

"Yeah." Elise took another sip. A little chink of concern rifled through her. Today was Wednesday. She needed to get back home soon in case Grandma Babe came early.

"Well, you sure have it sweet," Lavina murmured. "I don't know how you've always done it. You've always had people looking after you."

Elise smiled and shrugged as an answer.

The breeze picked up and ruffled the pinky-white blooms of the magnolia tree out front. Elise was watching the flowers when a police car turned onto the street. It quickly grabbed the attention of both women.

"Well, what's he driving all slow like that for?" Lavina asked.

They straightened slightly as the car stopped in front of the driveway.

Brad Carter stepped out, making his muscles flex as he shut the door. Elise sucked in her breath. He immediately tucked down the front of his shirt and pushed his shoulders back as he walked up to the steps.

Elise raised her eyebrows at Lavina and whispered, "Mmmm."

"Not bad, huh?"

"He looks a lot different from high school, that's for sure."

"Ten years and time spent in Iraq will do that to a person."

"Miss Lavina Chantly?" Brad asked, reaching the porch.

"Why, hello there, Detective Carter," Lavina answered in a smoky voice. "You drop by for a glass of sweet tea?"

He cleared his throat, his gaze taking in Elise for a moment, then back to Lavina. "I have a few questions I'd like to ask you."

"Brad Carter, we've known each other since we were both knee high to a grasshopper. Why are you acting so formal? Pull up a chair and sit for a while." Lavina smiled.

Brad scratched the back of his neck before flipping open a notebook. "Just cooperate with me, Lavina. You were always so talkative before. Did you know you were in line to inherit over a million dollars of Mr. McMahon's estate?"

"Oh, poo. I don't care about that. But, if it's talking you want, there's a place I know that would be just perfect to talk with you." Lavina lifted an eyebrow provocatively.

Brad cut his gaze to Elise again. "Focus, Lavina. Where were you on the night of the 27th?"

Lavina's mouth dropped open, and Elise's did too. What was Brad suggesting? And why?

10

Elise balanced herself against the porch railing outside Mrs. Campbell's house and stretched her legs. "Another day, another dollar," she murmured. She'd just collected all three dogs who were now tugging in different ways. "Y'all hold your horses. Just a sec." She stepped on all three leashes to free up her hands so she could scoop her hair into a ponytail. A vision of Wilma Rudolph—the amazing athlete who overcame polio to become the world's fastest runner— swept through her mind. She nodded grimly. If she can do that, I can definitely get this 5k done.

Just then, Frodo tugged hard on the lead, knocking her off balance. She staggered forward trying to stay afoot as the dog darted behind her. Across the street, the neighbor stared at her curiously.

Elise gave the neighbor a quick wave to let him know she was okay. Her face flushed. Curly from the Three Stooges replaced her daydream.

Shaking her head, she pulled up the music list on her phone and hit play. After jamming in the earbuds, she hit the sidewalk with a smooth stride that somewhat saved her dignity.

She was going to Ford Park.

It was her first time back since the train accident. The dogs jogged by her side with tails wagging. In only a few minutes, her muscles had warmed up and her stride became more natural.

There was something hypnotic about running. Each step felt like a heartbeat. One more, one more, one more, as her ponytail flipped back and forth. She took a deep breath in and reached into her pocket to thumb up the music volume.

The morning air felt cool against her face and smelled like clover. She'd missed this, all those years living in New Hampshire with her husband. Mark's face swam in her mind, and she squashed it down with a shudder. Instead, she let her memories draw her back to a time when she was a little girl, running out the door to Lavina's house. Every morning, they'd meet and walk to school together, and every weekend found them exploring this very park.

She was going to get Vi off the hook. Thinking back to Brad's questioning, she'd seen Vi's face flash the same broken look as back when her mother died when she was a little girl. So confused and hurt.

Elise's mouth tightened with determination. There was no way she'd let her friend be the fall-guy.

How could anyone really think Lavina could have killed Cameron anyway? All throughout her school years she'd garnered a reputation being the first to take up for the underdog. Everyone liked Lavina.

The question echoed over and over with the drum of her feet on the sidewalk.

Up ahead was the park sign, complete with its hand painted bear done in the early 50's. The dogs strained even harder on their leads at the smell of the water. Even the Pekinese was pulling ahead.

Considering how early it was, she was surprised by the number of people already at the park. One walked his boxer, who growled as they ran by. A little further, a man cast his fishing line into the water dotted with white reflections from the clouds above. Neither person looked up as she passed.

Her pulse thumped in her neck, and she unzipped the front of her jacket to cool down. Her thigh muscles burned. The halfway song began on the iPod and spurred her to pick up the pace. She needed to press on just a little bit more, and she'd pass the first point of fatigue. Just push through.

Barely visible up ahead was the car lot and the train tracks.

Where Cameron died.

Her forehead broke out in sweat.

Now, the edge of the parking lot was in view. First a busted curb and then faded white lines marking out parking stalls. A row of used cars still waiting for their turn to be run through the service station sat by the end of the building.

Most likely all trade-ins.

Elise slowed to a stop, ostensibly to give the dogs a break. She linked her hands behind her head to catch her breath and stared up at the sky. It was going to be another hot day. The dogs flopped down in the shade of a large maple tree with their tongues hanging out.

Finally, heart rate slowing a bit, her gaze traveled to the line of cars. All of them were dirty, some marked with painted numbers on the windows.

Something felt off, and she looked again.

One of the cars had its trunk popped open.

She glanced around to see if anyone was nearby. "Come on, pups," she called. The dogs stood panting, then the four of them entered the lot. Frodo's nose immediately went to the ground sniffing.

Her footsteps crunched loudly on the gravel, making her shiver. It was creepy being here with it so empty and quiet. She hurried her way over to the car.

It was a newer Ford Taurus. Fresh scrapes in the blue paint dug down to the silver on the outside of the trunk. The lid now sat half-cocked, unable to be shut completely.

She peered inside and could just see a puddle of water darkening the carpet from where the rain had leaked in.

Who did this? Did someone want their old car back, or did they leave something behind in it?

Leaning in closer, she saw the corner of what looked like a rippled, wet stack of papers just to the side of the puddle.

If only the trunk were open just a bit more.

She covered her hand with a corner of her shirt and tried to lift the trunk. Despite the damage, the latch held firm and refused to budge.

Sighing, she released it and brushed her fingertips on her leg. A flutter and caw overhead from a crow made her flinch. Warily, she looked around the lot. Still no one around. She turned back to the path and scanned the area to locate where Cameron had been hit by the train.

It was unmistakable. All the debris had been cleaned up, but nothing could hide the long, black gash marring the bank from where the Mercedes had been pushed by the train.

Did Frank do this? Somehow, in a fit of jealousy, did he poison Cameron, strapped him in the driver's side of his car and parked it across the tracks? But, how could a skinny man like Frank force Cameron to ingest poison? Elise frowned, unable to see that happening. She pulled out her phone again and groaned to see that the playlist was almost over.

Biting the inside of her lip, she scrolled for Brad's name. She had to tell him about the trunk.

He answered on the first ring. "Hello?"

"Hi, Brad. It's Elise."

A pause for a second, then, "Oh, hey there. What's going on? Need an emergency Lucky Charms run?"

"Oh, you're so funny. Listen, I'm just out jogging and came across something weird. You have a minute?"

"I'm filling out some paperwork right now, but I can swing by your place in about twenty."

"You know where I live?"

He laughed. "Hey, it's a small town. When a big city girl comes home, word gets around."

"Whatever. I'll see you then." She hung up and realized she was smiling. "Come on kiddos," she called to the dogs. "First one back gets two doggy treats."

11

Elise brought the three dogs in through the gate into her backyard. Once released from their leashes, they all made a beeline for the water tub she'd already set out under the old tulip poplar. She hurried inside for the promised dog treats. On her return trip, she nearly tripped over the orange tabby who'd suddenly appeared at her ankles.

"Back again? Where'd you come from?" She sat on the bottom step to scratch the cat's back, frowning as he felt thinner still. "You're a good boy. Aren't you?"

The cat rubbed his cheek against her hand before standing up with its front paws on her knee. He stretched his nose toward hers. Automatically, Elise bent closer, and they touched noses. His whiskers tickled her cheek. "You are a sweetie pie. I have a treat for you." She carried him into the house, the screen door squeaking as it closed behind her.

After a mad search through the cupboards, she located where she'd stashed the cans of cat food. Stacked them right with the tuna fish. She shook her head as she set the can on the floor. "That would have been a nasty surprise for me, let me tell you," she assured the cat.

He sniffed the food and moved away.

"Oh, that's right. You like to eat alone." She rinsed her fingers and moved into the bedroom to check her hair. Just outside the doorway, she took a backward peek.

The cat had his face buried in the can.

Smiling, she redid her ponytail, frazzled from the earlier jog. Then she drummed up the Key Center half-marathon on her phone.

Her heart pounded as she read the description. Thirteen miles through the city. Could she do it? Could she really do it? When had she last really done something for herself? Spurred on by adrenaline, she scrolled for the application and quickly filled it out. Her thumb wavered over the "submit" key.

Elise jumped at the sound of a car in the driveway. She ran to the window and caught sight of Brad walking up the steps. Wimping out, she backed out of the marathon page.

Outside on the porch, he paused for a second. Then knocked soundly.

She opened the door with a smile. "Hi, there."

"Hi. Sorry, I'm late." He smiled as his hand tracked through his hair. "This investigation is taking more time than I expected."

"Sorry to bother you. You know, I could have just told you over the phone."

He cleared his throat. "After seeing you at Lavina's, and running into you earlier, I felt like we needed to catch up. Really, I just wanted to see you again. I can't believe how you still look the same. Wow. This is getting awkward isn't it?" He half-heartedly laughed and took a step back.

Elise laughed too and held the door open. "Come on in. I'll make some coffee. You hungry?"

"I mean if you're not busy." His gaze fell to her yoga pants and lingered.

"No. I have stuff to tell you, remember?" The cat, snubbed by her inattention, stood up and stretched against her leg. Elise's eyes flew open as he sank his nails in a tiny bit. "Ow! Cat!" She shooed him away and stepped back so that Brad could come in.

"Nice place," he murmured, looking around the living room. He walked to the couch and touched the pink afghan she'd left over the arm. "You make this?"

"I did, but don't be too impressed. It took me like two years." She chuckled as she tucked her hair around her ear. "Anyway, this house has been a good place for me. I've always loved this neighborhood. It's funny how Miss Alice still lives down the street."

"Yeah, she does. Not a lot changes around here." He squatted and reached out a hand to the orange tabby.

The cat narrowed his eyes before stalking off with his tail in the air.

"Don't take that personally," Elise hollered as she made her way to the kitchen. She waved him to follow her. The dark wood floors reflected the sun from the many windows, making the room feel light and airy. "He keeps appearing on my doorstep night after night."

The cat jumped up on the desk and watched her closely. She went over and scratched his head. Satisfied, the cat curled up and shut his eyes.

"Looks like he adopted you," Brad said.

"Maybe. I could use the company." Elise grinned, realizing how that sounded. She pushed over a mug of coffee. "Cream or sugar?"

"Nah, black is fine. So, what did you want to tell me?" He blew on it to cool it down and took a sip.

"I found something weird today. On my jog. It was at the back of the car lot—"

"You went to the car lot?" He interrupted as his eyebrows raised in surprise at her.

"Well, I was jogging around the lake."

"You have to leave the trail to get to the lot."

"There is a path there you know. It's well beaten down through the grass."

He looked up at the ceiling and sighed. "There's the Elise I remember. Continue."

"Well, one of the cars looked like the trunk had been forced open."

"Tell me you didn't touch it."

"Not with my hands." She held them out as if to prove they were clean.

"Elise." He sighed again. "We'll probably have to take you down to the station and fingerprint you so we can eliminate your prints."

"I didn't touch anything! I used my shirt!" she insisted.

He rolled his eyes. "You're not exactly helping here."

She marched toward the fridge and yanked open the door. She pulled out the mayonnaise and lunch meat, giving him a guarded look as she slapped them on the counter. "You want something to eat or not?"

His gun holster made a leather squeak as he sat on the bar stool. "Yeah, sure. Listen, I'm not trying to give you a hard time, but this is serious stuff. I know you care about Lavina and want to help her, but you can't go running off and get yourself involved."

"I was careful. It was very strange."

"What made you curious about it?"

"There was a fresh scrape from where the paint was scratched off. And one corner of the trunk was still pretzeled up." She spread mayonnaise on the bread and folded on the pastrami. "This is from Lavina's Deli. You want mustard?"

He shook his head. She ripped off a paper towel and slid the sandwich over to him. Humming, she began to make a new one.

Brad took a bite with a thoughtful look. "I went over that car lot with a fine tooth comb, and didn't see anything like that."

"I guess somebody wanted something in there, and they wanted it bad. Something important."

"How do you know it wasn't a random car thief?"

Elise bit the inside of her cheek, thinking. "There were more expensive cars on the lot. Why wouldn't the thief had gone for them? And who breaks into a car, but leaves it? They had to be looking for something."

He finished off his sandwich and wiped his mouth on the paper towel. "Thanks for lunch. And for giving me more work to do."

"You leaving now? Where are you going?"

"Out to the dealership. Maybe a rain check for another coffee?"

She nodded.

"And I'm serious about maybe having to fingerprint you. Do me a favor and stay out of trouble."

She followed him to the door and waved as he got into his car.

Back inside, the cat yawned, ending with a meow. Elise dropped a torn corner of lunch meat for him. Quickly, she packed the fridge back up. "Maybe I'll just head over there," she told the cat. "He might need help finding the car."

He blinked coolly at her and jumped down from the desk to sniff the meat.

She bit her lip, thinking, before snatching her keys.

Stooping to give the cat another scratch, she whispered, "And you, my friend, really need a name."

As she was putting her key in to lock the door, she caught sight of her neighbor hauling his lawnmower out of his garage.

"Hey!" she yelled.

He pushed his hat back and looked around.

"Over here!"

Spotting her, he walked over. "You our new neighbor?"

"Yes." She stuck out a hand. "Name's Elise. Do you know anything about an orange tabby? He's been hanging out at my back door since I moved in."

"My name's Thomas." He inspected his hand for dirt and brushed it off before shaking hers. "I guess you've met Max."

"Oh, I was wondering what his name was. Who does he belong to?"

"He used to belong to the people who lived here. They must have dumped him when they moved."

Elise felt her face heat with fury. Swallowing hard, she answered, "Some people.... Wow. I guess he doesn't have to worry about that anymore. He's got a home now."

"Don't get me started. Anyway, welcome to the neighborhood."

"Thanks. And, don't worry about all those dogs in my yard. I'm just dog-sitting."

"Fine by me." He grinned, half-turning back towards the garage.

She gave him a wave and got into her car.

12

Elise exhaled deeply as she pulled in next to the police car and climbed out. A quick glance at her Fitbit showed her heart rate was elevated. She imagined Brad's face when she showed up—butting in again?

But she had to know what was in the trunk. It really felt like it was her clue.

The dealership had remained closed since Cameron's death. Row after row of brand new cars glinted like marbles in the sun. When were they planning to open again? Surely a business this big couldn't handle the financial loss of long-term closure.

She walked around the outside of the dark showroom. The windows—painted in screaming red letters 'SALE'— already looked like they could use a cleaning in just the twelve days since it had been closed. Angel Lake was known for its dust storms, and they'd had a few in the interim.

Elise rounded the back corner of the building and headed over to where the garage was. Here, the cars weren't so pretty. Several had their hoods up, waiting to be fixed, like time had been set to pause.

Still further back was the used car lot, and then the row where she'd seen the Ford with the jimmied trunk.

She could just make out a dark figure standing at the rear of the vehicle.

Brad looked up at the sound of her footsteps. He raised his hands beseechingly. "You really can't stay out of trouble, can you?" he called.

Elise shrugged and smiled as she came up beside him. "I told you I didn't touch the trunk. I just want to know what's inside."

He glanced at it. "This definitely is new. Good catch. I requested the forensic team to come back and check this out."

"A clue!" Elise made a half-hearted fist pump in the air.

"Yeah. This was good. Just don't make a habit of finding any more. Let me do my job. You know how this made me feel calling it in? A jogger discovered a clue that I should have found."

"Hey, you can't be everywhere all the time."

Brad touched the scraped paint with a glove covered finger. "Whoever did this was not too smooth about it. There are better ways to get in."

"Like how?"

"Like opening the driver's door and popping the trunk latch. The car wasn't locked. I'm gathering you didn't check?"

Elise's mouth dropped open. She shook her head.

"Good. That helps. Fewer fingerprints that way. Now, I just need to get my hands on the video footage from inside the dealership."

"What? Why aren't they just handing that to you?"

"Apparently, it's monitored by a third party. They aren't making it easy to see. I might have to get a subpoena."

"That's crazy."

"Yeah. Nothing is ever easy in investigations. Remember that." His gaze flicked over her face. "By the way, I like your hair."

"Oh!" She'd forgotten about the haircut. "Thanks. That reminds me, I heard something interesting while I was there."

"More interesting. Great. Let's hear it." He crossed his arms over his chest and smiled with an overly-patient expression.

"So, you know how those salon places are. Gossip central."

"Yeah. I actually love them. Lots of info that everyone is more than willing to give out. I should have scheduled a haircut for myself." His hand whisked over the top of his closely cropped hair.

Elise wrinkled her nose. "Not too much to cut there when you keep it military short."

"Old habits die hard. Anyway, continue."

"There was this man who popped his head in the salon looking for his wife. Sylvia. Do you know her?"

Brad nodded. "Frank's wife. Yeah."

"After he left, Carla mentioned there was a ton of bad blood between Frank and Cameron, and that was before Sylvia got pregnant. I've been hearing it's pretty common knowledge that the baby is Cameron's. And then," Elise's voice raised with excitement as she remembered. "Another gal mentioned that Frank was working with the exterminator, who had a big job across from the dealership just days before Cameron died." She swiveled around to locate the Wiggle convenience store.

"You'll try anything to get Lavina out from being a suspect, won't you?"

"I'm not making this up. It's what I heard."

"Thanks for the gossip, but Frank's already been on our radar."

"Oh. So that was a bomb of a clue."

"No, I appreciate it. You can tell me anything you hear, anytime. Just don't go busting in searching out stuff by yourself. Let us do that."

They turned together and began walking back to the showroom.

"What are you going to do now?"

"Just wait for the team to arrive. It might not be for a while. You?"

Elise checked her Fitbit for the time. "I have to return the dogs. They're still playing in my back yard. That's my job, for now, a dog walker. Actually, I love it."

"Seems like quite a change from the big city. How are you doing with all of that?"

Elise shrugged. "I don't think I was ever made for city living. My husband, being a corporate lawyer, was always gone. He used to get m—" she paused, trying to think of the right word. "He wasn't happy if I didn't attend events by myself. Appearances you know. Everyone there is about them." She laughed a little. "I did love dressing up, but really, it's only fun when there's someone by your side. But, honestly, I never felt more alone than in my marriage. I didn't know how to fix it."

She looked up and noticed Brad staring at her. TMI, Elise! Her face flooded with heat. "I'm sorry. That all just slipped out. Still healing, I guess." Unconsciously, her thumb felt for the empty place on her ring finger.

"It's okay. It's still fresh," Brad offered.

"It really is. It will be finalized in little over a week. And I'm sad about all the wrong stuff. Not so much about the marriage ending. I'm more sad about the dreams I had as a young girl that are being taken away with it. But really, they were destroyed the night I read the text."

"The text?"

"Yeah. That's how I found out. So cliche, right? Still, it was almost a weird, sick relief when I saw the text message because I finally knew what was wrong. Some girl asked him if they were still on for that night. He'd changed her name in his contacts to Steve, but I figured no matter what something was up when Steve wanted him to bring extra condoms."

She shook her head with a sad smile. "But that's what happens sometimes. And now I'm here. And I'm doing okay, really."

Brad nodded. "I had a hard time when I returned home from the Army. It's not easy leaving one life for another. But slowly, eventually, everything does fit into its place like it was the way it was supposed to be all along." He leaned over and patted her shoulder. The pats changed to a slow squeeze. "Sure, there are some 'not okay' moments, but it will work out. You're strong. Stronger than you think. And I'm glad you're here."

"Full circle, right?" She grinned.

"Sometimes you just have to know when to come home." He gave a final clamp on her shoulder. "Now get out of here and take care of those dogs. And stay out of trouble!"

13

Elise walked out of the bright sunlight and into the dark nail salon. It had been two days, and she still hadn't heard anything more from Brad about the trunk. She debated whether it would be out of line to give him a call. Squinting, she looked around the interior for Lavina.

It was her first time getting a manicure since she'd left New Hampshire, and she would have been quite happy to wait longer, but Lavina had been insistent in their phone call that morning. "I need a distraction and some girl time," she'd begged. "And, I'd love to hear more about Brad."

Elise winced at the memory. She already knew where Lavina was going with that. Her thumb went to the divot on her ring finger, sending a pang of sadness. She still hadn't heard anything from Mark after her lawyer sent over the documents. But, from the way everything was going so far, her lawyer had assured her it would all be over soon.

Definitely too early to be grilled about Brad. She wasn't ready to jump into anything yet, not for a long time. And darn Lavina for suggesting otherwise! She huffed.

"Hello, darlin'!" Lavina's cheery voice rang out from the back of the salon. Her face was half-obscured by a pair of overlarge super-model sunglasses.

From behind the front desk, a young woman with silky black hair pulled into a tight ponytail smiled. She fretted with a vase of flowers, rearranging the long stalks, then beckoned warmly with her hand to lead Elise back to her friend.

"Why on earth are you wearing those indoors?" Elise grumped as she sat in the chair next to her.

Lavina pulled the sunglasses partway down and peered over the tops. "Last night was a bit late in the making. Two bottles of wine and Mr. G." She smiled lasciviously. "And everyone knows glasses make all eyes appear fresh."

"Yes, but you can't see a darn thing."

"Pish. Who needs to see things when there are darlin' people to take care of it for you?" Lavina flashed her million-dollar smile at the young esthetician. The gal held up a pink bottle for Lavina's approval. Lavina reached for the polish and held it into the light, before nodding. "Sparkles. I love it."

The esthetician gently took Elise's hand and placed it in a bowl of warm scented water. "Five minutes," she directed with a deep accent.

The bell chimed again. Both women looked up.

A woman in a violet dress suit with a spray of flowers adorning her matching hat, waltzed in. An unhappy teenage girl trailed in behind her. "Pricilla. Stand straight, dear. What have I told you about a woman's posture?"

"Crystal," Lavina hissed through gritted teeth and even Elise stifled a groan. Only pompous Crystal could bring out that reaction in Lavina. The recently divorced socialite treated Lavina with the social acquaintance of a rival mob wife—overly polite to her face, but wouldn't stop to spit if she found her on fire. And, for some reason, things had really amped up between them this last year.

Crystal addressed them from the doorway. "My good-gracious. This place is buzzing today."

"You have an appointment?" Ada asked.

"Yes, of course. Two o'clock."

"Come this way."

Lavina groaned as Ada settled the newcomers at the table across from them.

Crystal arched her eyebrows in their direction. "Why, hello there. Seems you're both enjoying a girl's day out. Bless your hearts." She carefully removed her purse and placed it on the cushioned seat next to her. "Pricilla, you remember Miss Chantly."

“Ms.” Lavina corrected, before smiling in Pricilla’s direction. Pricilla bobbed her head with an air of boredom and reached for a People magazine.

“Too bad you didn’t invite us. We just got back from the hair salon. The four of us could have had a full-blown girl’s day.”

“Oh, come now.” Lavina shot back a tight grin. “It’s been some time since you’ve been called a girl.”

Crystal’s eyes barely flickered at registering the insult. “I hardly have time to hang with girls, with all the charity work that must be done.”

Ada gestured to the other esthetician, Kata, hurrying out from the back room at the sound of the door chime. “You help her.”

Kata quickly scurried over with a steaming porcelain dish of water and placed it before Crystal. With a nod towards the younger woman, Crystal placed her fingertips in the water.

Ada dried off Elise’s hands off with a towel. She quickly pushed back the cuticles.

Kata rolled the bottle of polish before gently adjusting Lavina’s hand. She applied the polish with even strokes.

“Well, it’s nice you’re getting a mother-daughter break,” Elise replied, hoping to defuse the tension.

"It's just so odd to run into you today," Crystal continued, ignoring her comment. "We were just talking about you. Weren't we, Pricilla, dear?"

The teenager barely looked up from her magazine. She quickly nodded and turned the page.

"I was so surprised to hear that Cameron was your father, Lavina. How long were you planning to keep that a secret from all of us?" Crystal dropped the bomb with a purr.

Lavina straightened her shoulders. With her free hand, she fished her lipstick out of her purse. After gliding the red over her lips, she sent a wide smile back. "Why would you care, dear?"

Crystal sniffed at the use of the term. "I thought we were close friends, Lavina." She smiled up at Kata, who had set a glass of sparkling water in front of her.

"I hardly think taking the same yoga class makes us close friends. By the way, your downward dog definitely needs some improvement."

"I hardly dare to ask why you're such an expert." Crystal took a delicate sip of water.

Lavina laughed. "Oh, honey. I'm an expert in all sorts of things. But it seems you lost your chance to ask Cameron about that. Being newly single and all."

Crystal slammed her glass down. The sound seemed to startle her into reining in her emotions, and she drew in a deep breath. "Could I get a napkin?" She smiled at Kata. Then, coolly she answered, "I believe we've all lost the chance to ask Cameron something. I hear your getting a new sibling? A new itty bitty who might be contesting daddy's will with you? By the way, have you been asked if you have an alibi?"

Lavina went visibly white behind her sunglasses. Ada turned towards Elise, having just finished the last few strokes of the clear top coat on Lavina's nails.

"Elise, darlin'. Do you care if we continue our day elsewhere?" Lavina's tone was cheery despite her countenance.

"Of course." Elise stood up, taking her hand from the esthetician. "Maybe another day," she said to Ada.

"Oh. Leaving so soon?" Crystal's face shone with victory. "That's too bad. I imagine it's so difficult to squeeze in a manicure with all the hours you put in waitressing. Nice to see you give yourself a rare treat, dear."

"I'm not a waitress. I own the deli. But, it's okay. At your age, we can't expect your memory to be perfect." Lavina pulled out a hundred dollar bill from her purse and set it on the table. "Thank you, Ada. It was a joy as usual. Please keep the extra as recompense for the uglier people you must deal with." And with that, she adjusted her sunglasses and glided out.

Elise followed, feeling slightly out of her league.

14

Lavina was tight-lipped as they left the salon and asked Elise to excuse her. "I feel a headache coming on. We'll have to do it another day, darlin'."

Elise gave her friend a hug. She drove home replaying the scene at the nail salon over and over. "This isn't going to get any better thinking about it," she muttered with a grimace. But something in the back of her mind wouldn't let it go…triggering her to pay attention.

What was it?

Something that nasty old Crystal said? Elise twirled her Fitbit, trying to remember. She glanced at the rubber bracelet and pushed the button. Her eyes widened when she saw how low the number of steps were that she'd taken. If she was every going to compete in the half-marathon, she'd better get a move on.

Her phone rang. "Hello?"

"Hey, Elise. It's Brad."

A smile skirted her lips before she could help it. "Hi, Brad. How are you?"

"I'm good. Staying out of trouble?"

"Always." The grin was getting bigger, darn it. "What's going on?"

"I figured since you are feeling so detectivish I better do something to keep an eye on you. Want to tag along while I go over some footage from the outside of the McMahon dealership?"

"You don't need to ask me twice. Yes!"

"Great! Want to meet in a half hour?"

"Where? At the dealership?"

"Not yet. Let's meet at the movie theater."

"Oh—kay."

He laughed. "Seriously, I'm going over an alibi for Frank. I'm a little smoother than that."

Fifteen minutes later, Elise ran inside the theater where Brad was already interviewing a concessions stand worker. She walked up just in time to hear the teen say, "Yeah, he was here. I recognize him." The teen handed Frank's photo back to Brad.

"You have something to say about him?" Brad asked.

The kid scratched at a zit on his chin. "He, uh. I bumped into him out in the hall about twenty minutes after his movie started."

"Was he getting snacks? Going to the restroom?" Brad asked, his pen poised above his notepad.

The kid shook his head. "Nah. He was coming from that way." He pointed toward the front door. "I told him he better hurry, man. Those first ten minutes of Zombies Bride are smoking. He just said he left something in his car."

"And then what happened?"

"He went back into the theater. I didn't see him again."

Brad closed the pad and reached into his pocket for a card. "Thank you for your time. Give me a call if you think of anything else. Here's my number."

The kid thumbed the card and nodded. Elise wondered how long before that card ended up in the trash.

They turned to go.

"Interesting." Elise grabbed the door. "Twenty minutes unaccounted for. And a motive."

Brad raised an eyebrow. "Easy there, detective. First, just gather the facts. Now, come on. They're probably ready for us at the dealership." He eyed her sweaty hair. "Let me guess. You ran here."

"Yeah, I'll meet you over there."

"Hang on. I can give you a ride."

"No, you go ahead." She showed him the Fitbit. "I'm training for the Key Center half-marathon." She laughed. "And, it hasn't been going well. But I'm trying."

He smiled at her and swung into his car. As he drove by, he blipped his siren making her jump. She could see him laughing and shook her fist at him.

A soft, happy feeling filled her as she bent to check her laces. It had been a long time since she'd had felt silly and free to have fun like that.

Elise switched on her favorite playlist. Her bare nails caught her eye, and the almost-memory whisked right around the edges of her mind. She tried hard to claim it but it skittered away. "Just think about something else. It'll come back."

Unbidden, another thought overtook her mind as she jogged along the sidewalk. Her soon to be finalized divorce. Her feet echoed her thoughts as they pounded against the pavement. Eight more days. Eight more days. She still hadn't heard from Mark since they'd separated, and that surprised her. They'd been solely communicating through their lawyers.

Their marriage hadn't started that way. That first year had actually felt like a real life fairytale. He'd been so attentive, so loving. Every morning had started with a kiss, his darkly whiskered face lightly scratching against hers. And the way that man could move in bed. She'd lay there gasping when they were through. He'd always laugh and tease that she was booting him out now that his job was finished.

The memory made her smile. They had good times, but did she ever really know him?

A red and yellow spatter of color waving in the weeds reminded her of all the flowers he used to bring home. Guilt flowers, she knew now. He'd acted so sorry when she'd said she was divorcing him, and promised everything to get her to stay. But part of her wondered if it was because his firm looked down on divorce and he was due for a promotion. No matter what, she knew she'd never be able to trust him again. And what kind of life was that for her? Or for him?

When the dealership came into view, she felt a wave of relief to be able to the put the memories away. Picking up the pace, she sprinted the last few blocks.

She didn't see Brad's car as she jogged through the lot. She continued to the showroom's cement steps and into the shadow made by the huge awning. After stretching a moment, she sat down and examined the time on her Fitbit. She was getting better.

"Hey, looking good." Brad's deep voice came from the top step where he was leaning against the pillar.

She jumped. "I didn't see you there. Where's your car?" He pointed to the rear of the building. She continued, "Who are we supposed to meet here?"

"The dispatcher said it was the new receptionist. A gal named Violet Wagner."

"Oh, the one that replaced Sylvia."

"Yep. And Eric." He stood resting with his leg up on a step.

"Eric? Is his mom Crystal?"

"Yeah. You know him? He's the car salesman and manager here."

"You'd think there'd be more than just one salesman."

"Yeah well, between Cameron and Eric, they had things covered."

Just then, a middle-aged woman stepped out onto the terrace, the glass door closing slowly behind her. She wore a surly look and was staring hard at the cell phone in her hand. Her voice was terse as she spoke. "Apparently, Eric has decided not to show up. I honestly don't know what to do now."

Brad straightened. "Violet Wagner?" She nodded, and he held out a hand. "Brad Carter from the Angel Lake Police Department. This will just take a couple of minutes."

Her face creased with worry. "I'm not sure I should let you in. I can't get a hold of Eric or Mrs. McMahon."

"All we're looking for is movement outside the building around the time of the accident. Both Eric and Mrs. McMahon have alibis, so they aren't at risk in any way. We just want to catch the person who did this. You might be preventing another murder." Elise noticed he kept his voice reassuring with just a touch of warning at the end.

Violet rubbed her temple with her hand. Shaking her head, she stepped back and opened the door. "Fine. Eric should be here, and since he's not, I'm making the decision. It's right this way."

The three of them walked to the far back office. The interior of the dealership was dark, and their steps echoed ominously. After leading them down a hall, Violet pushed open a door. "Right in there." She pointed to a desk covered in papers. A computer sat amongst the chaos.

Brad dragged a chair over and motioned for Elise to sit. Violet punched some commands in the keyboard and then turned the monitor towards them.

"This is the pause, and here is rewind and fast forward." She pointed at the symbols on the number pad.

Brad pushed play. The screen split into four shots from each of the different cameras. Nothing moved in any of the shots. He pressed fast forward and leaned close to study them carefully.

Nothing happened.

One hour later, Elise was pacing in boredom by the vending machine in the lobby. Violet came over shaking a handful of coins. "Here." She offered them out.

"Oh, I can't take your money."

"Don't worry. We keep a jar of coins specifically for customers who are on the hook. Get yourself something. I'm gathering he's not having any luck?"

Elise plunked in the coins and pushed the option for iced tea. "Not so far."

"Well, that's good then, isn't it?" Violet gave a hesitant smile before disappearing back into her office.

Elise carried the drink into the back room that now felt hot and stuffy.

Brad still stared just as intently at the screen.

She sank into a chair and spun it with her foot, then leaned forward to grab a letter opener and attempted to clean out under her nails.

"Put that knife down and come over here."

Elise smirked at Brad's dramatic tone. She tossed the opener on the desk and rolled the chair over. "What did you find?"

"Check this out." He pushed play. After a minute, he clicked pause. "You see what I see?"

"Are you kidding me?" Elise reached over Brad's shoulder and scrolled the mouse to rewind. They watched the scene again.

The resolution was fuzzy, but in the bottom left corner, the camera caught the figure of a man in a hat, dark overcoat and glasses. The man was there only an instant before disappearing around the corner of the car dealership building. The time stamp was 12:32.

"Jackpot, baby!" Brad leaned back in the chair with his hands twined behind his head.

"Is that Frank?"

Brad shook his head. "Too short to be Frank."

"Sylvia?"

"Looks a mite thin to be Sylvia."

The two looked at each other. Between them, Brad's cell phone began angry vibrations.

"Hello?" He frowned at whatever was being said. "Great. I'll be right down."

His fingers flew over the keyboard, and then he turned to Elise. "Just sent that loop to myself, and I'll get the surveillance company to send the rest. Next, I'll go to the convenience store and check out their video footage too. It's from the wrong angle, but you never know. There's got to be more footage of this guy somewhere."

Brad touched her arm. "Listen, you need to be safe. Don't tell anyone what you saw here today. It could get back to the wrong person. I don't want you to get hurt."

"Don't worry about me. I always follow the number one rule in investigating, Detective Carter. Don't get hurt." But she knew right away who she was going to tell.

15

After they had separated from the car dealership, Elise texted Lavina asking her to come over that afternoon. In the meantime, she'd gathered Frodo, Horace, and Winnie and finished out her run.

When she arrived home, Lavina was already parked in her driveway waiting for her. As Elise unlocked the front door, words flew out of Lavina's mouth like she was trying out to be an auctioneer. "I'm so glad you called. I've been dying to talk to you. I've really made a mess of things now. I really did. Oh, hello cat. New?"

"That's Max. Down, Max. Down. He's worse than a dog."

Lavina ran the tips of her nails along his back with the barest touch. The cat stared at her with adoration. "Well, he seems to like me." She looked at her black pants with a frown.

"I'll keep him off of you. Max come here, already." Elise scooped the orange up and sat with him on her lap. He sprang from her and stalked off unhappily. "So, what's going on?"

"You first. No, never mind, me first. I can hardly stand it. Oh! The mess I'm in! So, I ran into a young lady we both know."

Elise waited, not even able to hazard a guess.

"Sylvia. Oh, Elise! I think she might be working with me at Sweet Sandwiches. And, she may be moving in!"

Elise's jaw dropped. Lavina, despite some hardships growing up, was never known to share. There was a good reason why Elise had her own place now instead of bunking in with her best friend. "How on earth did you let that happen?"

"I couldn't help it. My mouth just went and said it before I could stop it."

"For crying out loud, Lavina. Don't say things like, "my mouth" like it's some crazed preschooler at its first Easter egg hunt who just found the stash of eggs. You're the one who controls it."

"Well, there it is. Apparently, I'm going to have a new roommate." She looked imploringly at Elise. "Help."

"What exactly did you say?"

"I said that she wasn't alone, and if I could help in any way with a job or a place to stay to let me know."

"And what did she say back?"

Lavina fiddled with the cuff on her blouse. "She said she'd let me know if she needed anything."

"Well, that hardly sounds like she's ready to move in. You supported her. I wouldn't worry yet. But next time, pause before you blurt." Elise relaxed back in the couch.

"That's a good word." Lavina grabbed her phone. "I'm tweeting that."

"So, now I have a secret. Today, I saw a suspect on the surveillance tape at the car dealership." Thrill shot through her at the memory. She grabbed the dog brush from the side table and began running it through Frodo's fur.

Lavina made a face. "You have to do that here?"

Elise eyed the hair floating in the air that Lavina made a show of fanning away. "You're right. Let's go outside." She called the dogs who followed her obediently.

Although small, the backyard was filled with bright sprays of color. Orange lilies bobbed in clusters. A spindly plum tree had lost its flowers and was now decorated with hard green fruits. Purple irises lined the back fence.

Lavina stared hard at the weathered picnic bench before she gingerly settled herself upon it. She slid her sunglasses onto her face. "You viewed surveillance tape? Oh, you and Brad—"

Elise patted Frodo's back end to get him to sit. The dog smiled at her with tongue lolling. "You like this don't you," she murmured, before addressing her friend by holding out her ring finger. "Quit trying to ship me off. It didn't work in high school, and it sure as heck isn't going to be something now."

"Pfft." Lavina was not impressed. "I don't see a ring on it."

"Yeah, but it's going to be a long, long while before I'm even ready to think about it again."

Lavina smirked behind her sunglasses. "Oh, you're thinking." She leaned forward and gave Elise a hard look. "Speaking of thinking, have you thought about Botox?"

"Botox? I'm talking about a guy I saw on video the same day Cameron was killed!"

"Never too early to do preventive care," Lavina chided. She appraised her friend with a critical eye. "Something you should really be thinking about."

"Oh my gosh, Lavina. Only you could turn a murder suspect discussion into a beauty tip session."

"I'm just saying you're not getting any younger," Lavina said drolly. She looked at her nails. "So, tell me what you saw."

Elise frowned. "Admittedly, it's not very impressive. A tall man with a wide-brimmed hat pulled low. Long jacket. Glasses."

"Any suspects?"

Winnie nosed up under Elise's legs. She gave her a friendly scratch then turned back to grooming Frodo. "Maybe. Nothing really solid."

"Well, I have a thought. Have you considered Mr. Davis? He wears glasses and long coats."

"He's paralyzed."

"No, I don't think he is. We'd never heard a diagnosis, just that he'd been badly hurt in the accident. I always thought that he was playing possum."

"He does have the motive."

"Because, if he can really walk, that's quite deceitful."

Elise shrugged. "It's not against the law to be able to walk. But one thing has been running through my mind."

"What's that?"

"I'm worried it could be Sylvia. The person was tall, but she could have accomplished that with heels. And she has the most to gain. " Elise ran the brush through the dog's thick fur a few more times. Still deep in thought, she cleaned the brush.

Lavina straightened on the bench. "I hardly think that's the case. I can't imagine how a woman could make herself look like a man. And why would she want to implicate Mr. Davis anyway? He's the one known to wear glasses. No. It had to be him. Either that or some other man."

"Well, I don't know. You couldn't really make out any facial features. It really could have been anyone."

"If he could have been anyone, then he might as well be no one, and you should just throw that clue out.

Honestly, it had to be him because it's too coincidental. Has it ever been ascertained that he was at the therapy place on the day of Cameron's death?"

Elise shook her head.

"Exactly. And, why was he at the funeral? Probably to gloat. My, oh my. It's so hot out here, it feels like there's nothing but a screen door between here and hell." Lavina fumbled through her purse, pulled out a pamphlet and waved it in front of her face. "Are you almost done, sweet pea? I really can't take a second more of this."

"How can you be so hot when you're always taking vacations to Tahiti with Mr. G?"

"Why, Elise." Lavina's bottom lip curved ever so slightly into a smile. "Those vacations are fueled by many martinis, king size beds, and air conditioning. All of which could be yours if you would just take proper care of yourself." She snapped the paper shut and returned it to her purse. "Now let's go inside. I'm tired of the sun and haven't brought my sunhat." She inspected a freckle on her arm. "I do need to brush up on my tan, though. Speaking of Tahiti, don't forget about our cruise in a couple of months."

"We can't go. You might miss the reading of the will."

Lavina sighed. "That man has caused me nothing but trouble. Even in death! I don't care about the will. In fact, I hope he leaves me nothing."

"It doesn't work that way. No matter what, the kids and the wife split it 50/50 according to state law."

"Well, la-di-da. I guess I'll let my tax consultant deal with it."

"You're pretty relaxed about the possibility of inheriting a million dollars. If you need help spending it, let me know. In fact, I think you better consider me as one of your charity cases."

Lavina stood up, hands scrunched together. Elise had thought her last comment would've made her laugh, but instead Lavina looked as if she might cry. "Honestly, I just want to be left alone about it. I can't wait until this whole thing is over." She walked into the house.

Elise watched her leave with concern. Frodo bumped her hand as his tail thumped against the flagstones. "You ready to go in, too? Just look at all this hair. I think there's enough for another dog, you funny boy." Frodo pranced excitedly. Winnie and Horace joined the bouncing. All three knew a treat was in store since the grooming was over. "All right, let's go in check on Lavina. Maybe, I'll suggest we go shopping for a new bathing suit. That should cheer her up."

The dogs scampered ahead of her up the stairs and pressed themselves against the screen door. Elise hurried, afraid the dogs might push the screen in.

But deep inside she was worried, very worried. What other secrets was her friend keeping?

16

Elise sat straight up in bed gasping. She had that dream again. The dream where the train smashed into the car.

Loud, screaming, tearing metal. And the side of the road was lined with vases of flowers.

But, finally, she knew what she'd been reminded of at the nail salon.

Sitting on the desk had been one of those vases filled with the same flowers.

She leaned over to the end table and reached for a pad of paper, quickly scribbling.... "Call nail salon tomorrow and check where they came from." She looked at the words for a moment. Was the sender the same one who sent them to the funeral? She thought about the stalks of bell-shaped flowers. They'd also been the same ones she'd seen at Mrs. Campbell's house. Why choose those flowers?

Puzzled, she set the pad down and lay back in bed. It might be a long night.

* * *

The next morning, Elise woke up like a live wire and nearly sprang out of bed. The urgency to call the salon energized her more than any cup of coffee ever had. She glanced at the Fitbit and groaned. Seven thirty. Way too early for the salon to be open.

She padded out into the kitchen and added water to her coffeemaker. Max had followed her from her room and now meowed by her feet. He arched his back to stretch. Elise quickly stepped away from him. She knew what his next move was—to stand up against her hip and poke his claws in. "For a vagabond, you sure aren't very patient for your food."

She found his canned cat food and pulled off the lid. "Last can, hmmm."

He looked away from it when she set it down, seemingly disinterested. "Yeah, whatever." Elise ignored him and poured herself some coffee. As soon as her back was turned, the cat sauntered over to the can. Elise watched him from the corner of her eye. He sniffed the food. Elise smiled. "Caught you!" He immediately blinked huge green eyes at her and began grooming his tail.

Elise laughed and took her mug to the window seat. This was her favorite part of the old house. A bed of bookshelves topped with a thickly padded white cushion made the base of the seat. Directly outside the window grew a cherry plum tree. She curled up on the cushion and balanced her mug on top of her leg.

Who was the figure in the video just before Cameron died? The thing most apparent to her was that the man hadn't been headed in the direction Cameron's Mercedes had been found, or from it either. Instead, the figure looked as though he were headed for the side door by the financing office.

And, if not Mr. Davis, then who? Frank had a similar body type to the figure, but he had produced a movie ticket stub for that exact time. And someone in the theater had vouched that they had seen him. But why was he gone for those twenty minutes? Was that really enough time to get to the dealership and back?

Tall, thin, and a hat. Lavina was right. It could have been anyone.

Elise checked her Fitbit for the time again and decided to get her run in. The morning was cool, and she had nothing better to do. She quickly dressed in her yoga pants and tank, then slid on the armband to hold her phone. "I feel like I should be in a James Bond movie with all this gear on," she told Max, who britted back at her. "All right, I won't forget. Cat food." After swooping her hair into a ponytail, she locked up and was off.

* * *

This morning, her run took her up the Old Farm Road, an older part of town. This was where Sylvia had once lived with Frank. She jogged past house after house, all built the same economical way—tiny two stories with four concrete steps leading to the same front door. Some were fenced in with chain link. Tall grass wove in between the links where they were in no danger of getting mowed. In one spot, a stalk of blue flowers braided itself in amongst the grass. Elise slowed her steps to look.

It was a different color, but it was the same flowers that had been at the funeral and the same ones at the nail salon. She pulled a blossom off and tucked it in the band of her shorts. It'd be smashed, but maybe she could still identify it when she got home.

She ran a finger under the Fitbit to loosen it and checked the time. Eight thirty. Just enough time to jog over to the salon and cool down on their entryway.

✽ ✽ ✽

At promptly nine o'clock, Ada walked over to the salon's window and flipped the sign to OPEN. Dressed in her usual pink smock, she had a big smile as she opened the door. "Come in! You have an appointment?"

Elise still felt flushed from her run. "No, not today. I have a funny question, and I was in the neighborhood so I thought I'd just stop by and ask." Her eyes burned at the strong smell of acetone that still lingered in the air.

Ada waved her in. "You like some water?"

"Yes. Thank you."

Ada hurried to the back and returned with a bottled water. Her white Keds squeaked on the floor. "Oh, so funny!" She grinned. "I just mopped."

Elise smiled back and cracked off the lid. She took a few hurried swigs as she looked around for the flowers.

They were gone.

Disappointment hit her hard as she screwed the lid back on.

Ada waited patiently, still smiling, obviously wanting to hear what she had to say. Pointing in the direction of the counter, Elise said, "I had a question about the flowers that were there the other day. Do you remember?"

"Oh! Yes! Over there?" Ada indicated the back wall where the flowers now stood.

"Yes!" Elise felt a rush of excitement. "Where did you get those? They're lovely!"

"Kata's husband sent them." Ada's voiced lowered several degrees. "He lost too much money at poker that night." She covered her mouth like a little girl and laughed.

"That's funny," Elise agreed. "What florist did they come from?"

Ada shook her head, confused. Trying again, Elise asked, "Do you mind?" At Ada's blank look, Elise delved in between the blooms to look for a card. Finding it, she pulled it out pinched between her index and middle finger.

A gold flower stamp decorated the top corner. Underneath in embossed cursive were the words, "Tamara's Fabulous Flowers." Elise pushed the card back among the baby's breath and wiped her hand on the side of her pants.

Tamara's flower shop? She'd never heard of it. She had to keep reminding herself a lot had changed since she left. Obviously, she didn't know the town as well as she used to.

Interesting.

Ada smiled at Elise with her eyebrows raised. "You find it?"

Elise nodded. "I sure did. Thank you so much. That made my day."

"You going to make a new appointment. For—" She flicked her gaze towards Elise's bare nails.

Elise looked down and resisted the urge to hide them. "I need to do that. Soon!" She headed toward the door. "I'll see you later, Ada!"

17

It turned out, Tamara's Fabulous Flowers was only four blocks away from the nail salon. Elise jogged there and was surprised at how much better her stamina was already, compared to just a few weeks ago. She couldn't help grinning in satisfaction as she pushed open the door.

A cute bell jingled overhead. Inside, the scents of fresh greens and heavy rose stirred around her, propelled by several floor fans.

The counter was empty. Elise stood for a few seconds before ringing the tiny bell next to the cash register. While she waited, she inspected the shop.

Brightly colored cards and balloons waiting to be filled with helium lined one wall. A hanging Ficus climbed from its planter and up around a window, before finally draping over a white garden statue. A stone fountain ran, its water bubbling cheerfully.

Elise walked over to look at it. At the bottom of the basin swam two blood-red koi fish.

"Can I help you?"

Elise turned towards the voice. A woman appearing to be in her mid-forties had emerged from the back room. Her hair was awash with dark curls, ostentatiously pinned back in an attempt to control them. But several curls sprang free from the hair clip like a grasshopper's antennas.

"Hi, there. I was just admiring what a beautiful shop you have. I'm assuming you are Tamara?"

The woman smiled. "Yep, that's me. And thank you! I've been here a year, and I love it. So, how can I help you?"

"I had a question about a flower arrangement I recently saw, that reminded me an awful lot of some flowers that were at a funeral."

Tamara's face grew sober. "Are you talking about Cameron's?"

"Yes. How did you know?"

"It's the only funeral I've done in quite some time. And that was an original request."

Elise nodded. "Yes. It was something like thirty vases. Filled with the same flowers."

"Twenty-nine vases. And filled with Delphinium."

"They were quite impressive. How on earth did you find so many of the exact same flower?"

"Usually, I have to order my flowers, but those grow like weeds around here this time of year. The valley is just filled with them. I've been running a special on bouquets made with them because they're so abundant."

"Oh." Elise felt a pang of disappointment. "So they were chosen because of the sale?"

"No. Oddly enough, those were specially ordered. Between you and me, I was surprised myself because they hardly seem like they are notable enough to honor the death of someone. But I made them look amazing with the faux silver basins."

"They really were breath-taking. Honestly, a real show stopper."

"Thank you. I'm so glad." Tamara smiled. "I wasn't there so that's nice to know."

"Would it be too much to ask who ordered them?"

Tamara bit her lip, seeming to consider the request. After a moment, she shrugged. "I don't see why not. I wasn't told to keep it private." She lifted her tablet from beneath the counter and scrolled. Finding what she was looking for, she announced. "A Mr. E. Davis."

Elise blinked her eyes at the news. "Mr. Davis? With a local address?"

"He didn't give me his address, but I assumed he was local."

"Did you see him?"

"No. The order came in over the phone." She reached under the counter for some tissue paper and cutting shears. "That's how they usually come, unless it's a husband stopping by looking for an 'I'm sorry' bouquet." She laughed. "I sell a lot of those on Saturdays."

A smile winked across Elise's face in response, but her mind was spinning in another direction.

Why the heck was Mr. Davis sending flowers to the funeral of a man he was suing? And despised?

Elise made her goodbyes and headed back out to the street, just remembering she needed cat food. "At least I'm getting my steps in." She readjusted her ponytail and jogged for the store.

* * *

"Sylvia Nichols, what are you doing here?"

Elise looked up to see a middle-aged woman speaking to a heavily pregnant young woman.

The pregnant girl winced as she reached for the last package of diapers off the top shelf.

"What? Sylvia, are you just going to ignore me? Quit being ugly." The older woman's face flushed at the lack of response.

The diapers slipped back from Sylvia's reach.

"Well, that's a fine how-to-do. You better be more polite, Missy. As far as I can tell you are all on your lonesome. And it seems to me you are going to be needing all the friends you can get right about now."

Puffing, Sylvia stood on her tiptoes and heaved forward. Her big belly pushed in the bigger diapers on the row below and knocked two packages to the floor.

The older woman huffed in disgust and spun her cart around. Teetering on her high heels, she hurried out of the aisle.

"Can I help you? Here let me get that." Elise walked over quickly. Sylvia's eyes flickered with wariness, and she shook her head no. Ignoring her, Elise grabbed the diapers. "Slippery little suckers, aren't they?"

Sylvia licked her lips. Her skin was dry and flaky, and her blonde hair hung in dark hanks. She pulled her sweat jacket around her but it wouldn't reach across her pregnant stomach. "Thank you," she whispered. As she took the diapers, her shoulders hunched protectively forward, reminding Elise of a kicked dog.

"You don't have too much longer, do you?" Elise smiled, hoping to encourage the young woman.

"Just a couple of months until the real nightmare begins," Sylvia muttered and tossed the package into the cart. Two cans of soup rolled into a stack of top ramen.

Elise picked up the diapers that had fallen and replaced them. "I'm sorry things have been so hard."

"You have no idea."

Elise hardly knew the young woman, but she'd already grabbed her heart. Anyone could see that she was struggling. Elise knew that Frank had kicked her out, and she was sleeping at her mom's place, a hard woman known in the past for being quick with the back of her hand. And, to top it off, she'd lost the best job she probably ever had. Suddenly, Elise could see why Lavina had practically fallen over herself trying to help the poor girl out.

"I'm sorry about you and Frank. I'm going through it myself. Just wanted to say I can understand somewhat."

The young woman's gaze flicked back at Elise, and she started to say something. Instead, her eyes puddled up.

"Aww, honey." Elise automatically reached out to give her a hug, but Sylvia backed away.

"I'm fine. I don't need no charity."

"It's going to get better. You're due to inherit something from the will, you know."

Sylvia gave her a disgusted look.

"I know that won't make everything all right, but it will help. You'll be able to get your own place."

"Why on earth would I want my own place? To take care of this baby all by myself? I need my mama. Who else is going to help me in case this baby has colic?"

"Aww, I'm sure your baby will be real sweet."

"Sweet. I've heard sweet before." Sylvia raised her voice high in mock sarcasm. "At eighteen, it was, 'Look at that young Frank. Ain't he sweet?' 'Y'all should get married, that will be real sweet.' 'When ya going to have a baby and make a sweet family?' So far all those sweets have been like chocolates—all pretty with a bow. But every one I pick is the one I want to spit out." She fiddled with the diapers in her cart. "You have a sweet day now, ya hear?" She walked away on swollen feet.

Elise turned away too, her heart feeling heavier than ever. She could relate all too well to a few of those "sweets."

18

Elise knew the mailman came early in the morning. So she was surprised when she arrived home that night to see a package sitting on her step and mail sticking out of the house mailbox. Mailmen were not known to change their schedule, not in a small town like Angel Lake where the postman still went on foot on some of his routes. She wondered what caused him to be so late.

After climbing out of the car, she looped the three grocery sacks on her arm and walked to the mailbox. It was all junk mail addressed to "Resident."

Bending down, she inspected the box. This was addressed to her and taped well with brown packing tape. She picked it up and shook it a little. The weight shifted and she could hear a muffled rattle. Her lips pressed together as she rifled through her purse for her keys. She unlocked the door and nudged it open with her hip while trying to keep a firm grasp on her groceries, junk mail, and the box.

An orange fireball darted through the doorway and exploded at her feet.

"Max!" Elise bit off a scream. She searched to make sure she didn't step on him as she shuffled to turn on the light and then moved into the kitchen. She didn't need to worry. He'd perched himself on top of the china cabinet and blinked calm green eyes at her.

Elise dumped the stuff on the counter. "You need to get down from there!" She pointed to the floor indignantly.

The cat ignored her. Leisurely, he smelled the decorative wooden trim along the top of the cabinet.

"Really, you don't belong up there!" Elise crossed her arms over her chest. The cat lay with its tail dangling over the edge like an orange duster.

Elise frowned before returning to the groceries to find something to tempt the cat. She unpacked the bags, noting a serious lack of anything other than cat food, cereal, and milk. With a sigh, she rifled through the fridge. Since when did her fridge get so empty? And when did the condiments multiply?

Since Grandma Babe went on vacation, that's when.

"This is what you get for being a single woman. You eat cereal for dinner and have nothing to bait the animals with to get them off your Great Aunt Louise's china cabinet," she muttered. This was the true reason women became cat ladies. They just couldn't be bothered anymore.

She opened a can of cat food and set it on the floor. He blinked at it disinterestedly.

Ignoring the cat, she meandered back into the living room and flopped onto the couch. The box caught her attention again. Who was it from?

The cushion shifted next to her as the cat jumped up. He bumped his head against her arm. A deep purr erupted from his throat. Absentmindedly, Elise scratched under his chin and pulled the box closer.

No return address.

She slid it open and pulled out a single sheet of paper.

"My Dearest Elise," were the first typewritten words.

She flipped the paper over, her eyes searching for the signature. Her breath sucked in as she found it.

"Mark"

Quickly she fastened up the box back up and pushed it under the coffee table. "I don't even want to know," she explained to Max.

Just then, her phone vibrated with a text.

We need to talk. EEE Lavina's text was short and to the point. She'd ended in their high school code for an emotional emergency.

Elise felt a swell of exhaustion rise up. She looked longingly at her bedroom; she really just wanted to put on a pair of pajamas and watch some reruns of Friends. Instead, she typed, Sure. I'll be right over.

Feeling more tired than she had in weeks, she collapsed back on the couch. Max purred deeply next to her. He nudged her hand for attention. She scratched his cheek, waiting for an answer.

I have wine.

* * *

"Lavina, what's going on?" Elise sat on the settee next to her friend.

Lavina shook her head. "Oh, honey, it's bad." She nervously brought her finger to her lip and chewed on the ragged cuticle.

Elise's heart ached with worry. She'd never seen Lavina as anything but put together.

"I have to go to the police station tomorrow and give a statement of where I was on the 27th. It's official now. I'm an actual suspect." She fiddled with the cord of her silk bathrobe.

Elise's eyes widened. "What do you mean?"

"I mean," Lavina took a shuddering breath. "I mean they've proven I have a motive."

"The will?"

Lavina shook her head and shrugged. "Maybe. They summoned my bank records." Tears began to gather at the corners of her eyes. "There's something I have to tell you."

Elise suddenly filled with that feeling that she didn't want to hear the next thing about to come out of Lavina's mouth. She counted to ten and blew out. "Okay. Tell me."

"I've had to pay a thousand dollars a month to Eric."

"Eric?" Elise gaped.

"You know, Crystal's son. At the dealership."

"And, why on earth have you been paying all that money to him?"

Lavina licked her dry lips. "He knew about Mr. G."

Elise shook her head. "So? So what?"

"You don't get it. Eric knew who he was. Mr. G...."

Lavina grew quiet. Elise was alarmed to see fat tears drip down her cheeks, leaving tracks in her foundation. "Elise, I can't make you understand, but I had no choice. If he'd come out with that information, Mr. G would leave me. I would have been ruined. My business would have been ruined."

Elise closed her eyes, trying to assimilate what her friend was saying. "Why in the world didn't you tell me he was extorting you? I'm your best friend. You can tell me anything."

"I was going to tell you. Then the news came out that Cameron was my father. I felt like I could barely breathe. Then Cameron died...." Her voice trailed off.

Elise stared at her friend. "Honestly, I don't know what I'm more upset about, that you kept all this a secret, or that you're dating a man who's very identity could bring down your business." She rested her hand on Lavina's arm. "I'm worried about you. Tell me who Mr. G is. We have to go to the police about this. "

Lavina stared up wild eyed with alarm. "I can't go to them! I can't even tell you who he is. No one must know!"

"But you have to know Eric's going to tell. You can't just keep paying him forever."

"I can! I have to!"

A cold chill ran down Elise's back. "Lavina, where were you on the 27th? You weren't at the spa after all, were you?"

Lavina covered her face with her hands. "It's over. I'm ruined. I was there, Elise. I was there."

"You were there?"

"I was the one you saw in the video."

Elise felt the whole room spin around her. She tried to suck in enough air to make sense of what her friend just said. In her mind's eye, she replayed the snippet from the video. A tall person, completely clad in an overcoat and glasses. She'd thought it had been Mr. Davis. But to now discover it was her best friend? "Why on earth were you there?"

Lavina collapsed against the back of the settee loudly weeping. "Oh, Elise! What am I going to do? They're going to find out! The cops are going to find out and think I did it!" Her speech cut off into broken sobs.

Almost on auto-pilot, Elise began to make comforting shushing sounds. She patted Lavina's back. "It's going to be okay. It's going to be all right. Calm down. We'll figure this out."

Lavina's shoulders were noticeably thinner through her Dior robe. Elise could see how the stress had been eating away at her friend. "You aren't going to jail. There has to be a way. Just tell me what you were doing there. What did you see?"

Lavina took another deep, hitching breath and began to calm down. Sitting up, she dotted at her face with a bit of twisted tissue she'd pulled free from her pocket. She sighed again. "The last few weeks, I'd been trying to talk some sense into Eric. He said he had pictures that he kept locked in a safe. I didn't believe him. Cameron was too nosy to let anyone use his safe without getting his finger in the middle of the pie. I'd talked with Sylvia, and she mentioned that every one of them had locking drawers on their desk. That was where she kept the payroll. So, during lunch. I went to search through his desk."

"How were you planning on unlocking the desk drawer?"

"I didn't get that far. I'd just come around the corner when I saw Eric leave. He was holding a briefcase, and I watched him put it in the back of a blue four-door."

"In the trunk," Elise said dryly.

Lavina nodded sorrowfully.

"The one I discovered on my run the other day."

"Yep. That's the one."

"You were the one who broke into it."

"Well, not me exactly. I told Mr. G. He had someone do it the next night."

"Oh, Lavina! Why didn't you tell anyone?"

"What was I going to say? Who would believe me?"

"Well, for one, did you realize that places Eric at the scene right before Cameron died! Did you ever think he might have been the one who did it?" Elise frowned. "He's a nasty enough guy. I'm sure we can figure out a motive?"

"His motive? I can think of one. Try the fact that his mama was trying to sleep with Cameron."

Elise's mouth dropped open.

"Yeah, and Crystal wasn't subtle about it either. She was calling him at all hours, like a cat in heat."

"How did you know about that?"

"Because Sylvia and I talked. She was tired of getting the cold shoulder from Cameron ever since her positive pregnancy test. She was about to let it all out."

"So…."

"So I think Eric set Sylvia up as the one who killed Cameron."

"Which he could have done if he'd killed Cameron himself."

"Exactly."

"Lavina…."

"No, Elise."

"We have to."

"Absolutely not. You are under best friend secrecy. You cannot tell Brad."

Elise sank into the settee like a weight of bricks had landed on her. Turning her head, she said, "Fine, then. Bring out the wine."

19

The next morning she woke feeling like her mouth had been stuffed with baby dragon training papers, and her head wouldn't stop ringing. She rolled over on Lavina's spare bed. "Please, please make it stop."

She was about to roll back again when she realized it was her cell that was ringing. After scrabbling for it off the night stand, she punched the answer key.

"Hello?" Great. Her voice sounded like she was talking through carpet wool.

"Elise? Is this a good time?"

Brad. She squinted at her Fitbit. Eleven o'clock. Stifling a yawn, she sat up. "Yeah, of course. I've been up for hours."

There was a chuckle. "I don't know if I quite believe you. Anyway. I was going to see about that coffee rain check. And I thought you might like to join me on another fun errand."

She rubbed her hands through her hair. "Sure. Give me an hour, okay?"

"See you at noon then."

* * *

They met at the Impresso Espresso. Knowing that everything Lavina had told her the night before was a secret, Elise felt guilty. She wondered if she should divulge what had happened yesterday morning on her dog run, and if that would ease her conscience a bit. "So, I have a confession." She sipped her coffee, watching Brad's reaction over the top of the cup."

He instantly looked wary. "Okay."

"So, did you know there was a huge display of flowers at Cameron's funeral?"

"I'd heard."

"Well, I discovered who sent them."

He lifted an eyebrow, patiently waiting. Almost nonchalantly, he took a bite of his giant oatmeal cookie.

"It was Mr. Davis. You know, the one Cameron was in the law suit with. Well, after I left the florist, I tried to meet up with him."

Brad started choking on the cookie. She watched with concern as he coughed. He waved her off when she made moves to stand to help him. After a moment, he scrambled for his coffee and took a few small sips.

"What?" he weakly sputtered.

"I said, I tried to meet with Mr. Davis. You know, to ask him about the flower pots," she continued defensively as he looked at her aghast.

"Why in the world would you do that?"

"I had to know. It's been driving me crazy."

"What part of 'this is police business, stay out' did you not understand?" he asked.

"You're always busy!" Elise frowned.

"I knew it was a bad idea to clue you in." Brad pushed back from the table and shook his head. With a groan, he rubbed his forehead.

"Well, it didn't do me any good anyways." Elise sighed. "He wouldn't talk to me. The guard told me I wasn't welcomed."

Brad still wasn't happy. "Did you tell him why you were there?"

"I didn't get a chance."

"The problem with your questions..." He leaned close and his clean cedar scent went straight to Elise's head. She swallowed hard. "Is that it gives the suspects time to think of answers by the time I come around and ask those same questions. So I need you to knock it off."

Elise nodded and grinned up at him innocently. She didn't want to tell him that Mr. Davis had already called and scheduled an appointment with her for the following day.

"I'm heading to the dental office right now to check on Sylvia's alibi. I know this is a bad idea, but do you want to tag along?" He smiled. Her heart fluttered at the ease of his smile. She was constantly feeling off guard with his attention. When had she last made Mark happy like that? Long before his affair. Stop dancing with those memories. She fiddled with her earring and nodded.

"Do you really suspect Sylvia? I mean, she's pregnant. I can't even imagine that."

"People have done crazier things with less motive. Pregnant, kicked out by her husband and losing her job with the baby's daddy? And the baby will receive a huge chunk of the inheritance under state law? Pretty good motive to me." They were out in the parking lot now and walking towards the cop car.

Elise frowned. "I just can't picture it. She seems like someone who needs a mom—lost even—not a calculated killer leaving her lover drugged up on the train tracks. Just the opposite, a sweet girl." Her voice trailed off at the memory of Sylvia snarling the word, "sweet" at her a few nights ago.

"I can honestly say I hope it's not her, but I can't rule it out. My job is to find out who did it. Now, hop in. We're riding in the beast today," Brad said, holding the door open for her.

"Oooh. Do I get to ride in your cop car?"

"Don't tell me you've never been in the back of one." His gaze darted over her as he laughed. "I'll never believe it."

She blushed. There had been that drunken streaking at midnight out on the football field. All of her cheerleading friends had done it as a send off to their senior year. The entire school expected it.

And, apparently, so had the sheriff's office. She cringed at the memory of her parent's faces when the cops drove her home covered in a blanket.

"I plead the fifth on the account that I was young and dumb once."

She jumped in and studied with interest all the instruments and computer screen panel. "Makes me feel quite official," she said as he climbed in.

"Just do me a favor." He shifted into gear and turned in the seat to watch as he backed up. His 5 o'clock shadow was apparent this close, and she dragged her eyes away.

"What's that?"

"Don't touch anything."

* * *

A few minutes later, they were outside the Sunshine Smiles Dental Office. Before getting out, Brad opened his tablet and read some notes. Elise turned to look away so she wouldn't notice how cute his reading frown was. Her thumb found the divot on her finger. One more week, she reminded herself.

They climbed out and walked on a path of black lava rock to the office.

Brad opened the door for Elise. The receptionist looked up as they entered, and her teeth flashed snowflake white with her smile.

"Hi, there. How can I help you today?"

"Hi...." Brad's eyes darted around looking for a name tag.

"Margaret," the receptionist supplied.

"Hi, Margaret. I spoke to you yesterday on the phone about a Sylvia Nichols? She had an appointment here on the 27th."

Margaret's eyebrows drew together in concern, and she reached for the scheduling book. With practiced skill, she paged back to the 27th and quickly ran her finger down the column. "Yes, I see it here at 11:15."

Elise felt her muscles relax at the news. She hadn't realized how anxious she'd been that Sylvia had an alibi.

"Well, now. That's strange," Margaret continued, pressing her finger to her bottom lip. "I have a slash next to it that shows she came in at a later time." She nodded. "That's right. She was late, and we had to reschedule for the next afternoon." She looked up at them. "It's policy to do that if the patient is too late, otherwise the entire day is messed up. Poor girl. She left here in tears. Just kept insisting that she'd made it for noon and not 11:15."

"Was she upset when she arrived?" Brad pulled out his tablet and began typing. "What time was it when she finally came in?"

"Oh," Margaret looked up at the ceiling, thinking. "I'm guessing at least thirty minutes late. Any earlier and we still try to work them in. We might have been able anyway and just run into lunch, but the doctor had an emergency appointment for that time."

"An emergency appointment?" Brad looked up. "Can I ask who?"

"That's funny. It's not on the books." Margaret shuffled through the pages before turning to the computer screen. The screen flashed brightly as she searched. Finally, she pushed back, looking slightly embarrassed. "I'm not sure who it was. I don't see a record of it. But I can remember distinctly that the doctor had been busy."

"Did you see who came in?" Brad asked.

"No, actually. Dr. Harris told me he would take care of it and to go ahead and take my lunch. And of course, when I came back, poor Mr. McMahon....It was a horrible nightmare." She blotted at her eyes. Elise watched carefully. There didn't seem to be any real tears.

Brad thanked her, and the two of them turned to go. Once outside Elise couldn't help looking across the street. Through the trimmed holly hedge she could just make out the car dealership. And the train tracks that ran along behind it.

20

The next morning at eleven o'clock on the dot, Elise arrived at Mr. Davis's house. The security guard stepped out from the gatehouse with his hand on his belt. Elise was taken aback to see a gun holstered there.

She quickly rolled down the window. "I'm here to see Mr. Davis. I have an appointment."

"Your name?" The security guard's face was blank.

"Elise Sanders."

He gave her car a hard look, even peering into the back seat before he reentered the booth. His face creased into a deep snarl like she was a drug lord about to drop a hit on his boss.

She watched him pick up the phone with her heart beating in her throat. Frowning, she leaned back in the seat and told herself to knock it off.

A moment later there was a clank, and the gate rumbled back on its track. His arm waved out the window telling her to go through. Elise let off the brake and rolled forward.

Old growth maple trees edged the driveway leading up to the house. Their leafy boughs arching overhead shielded the pavement from the sun.

The house itself was magnificent and nearly took her breath away. Large and white, it had been built with typical Southern heritage.

She slowed to a stop and eyed the building. A small movement drew her attention to the far left window where she made out a tall figure standing there. The curtain dropped.

Elise parked the car by the portico. With an uncomfortable feeling, she thought about Brad and hoped he wouldn't be too mad when he discovered what she'd done.

She took the white marble steps lightly, her head swiveling, completely impressed with the massive pillars that held up the roof. Nervously, she slid her finger under the Fitbit and gave it a small twirl before stabbing at the doorbell.

The heavy oak door opened silently. A young woman stood at the entryway wearing a prim blouse and black skirt. It took Elise a moment to place her—Mr. Davis's assistant. She was shorter than Elise remembered, and something about her looked different, but Elise couldn't put her finger on why.

"Come in. Mr. Davis is expecting you." She spun on her high heels and led Elise through the hallway with smooth, gliding steps. After a moment, the young woman paused and waved her hand toward the library.

Elise's gaze dropped to see Mr. Davis in his chair just inside the doorway. The same plaid blanket covered his thin legs.

Mr. Davis coolly eyed Elise. With a flick of his wrist, he pushed the wheelchair back from the door. "I'm surprised you accepted my invitation after you were so rude as to drop by unannounced yesterday."

Elise felt her insides shrivel at his harsh demeanor, but she thrust back her shoulders. With a smile pasted on her face, she stepped over the threshold.

"I'm truly thankful you made time for me, Mr. Davis. What a beautiful place you have here," she murmured, craning her head back as her gaze traced a painted trail of flowers swirling along the archway.

"Follow me," Mr. Davis said pushing himself farther into the room. His wheelchair wheels hissed against the marble floor. "That was Estelle at the door."

"Estelle?" Elise dragged her gaze from the artwork to cut him a questioning look.

"My niece. Also my nurse and personal assistant. She's lived with me for the last ten years." He indicated his chair with a hand and a small shrug. "Truly the most loyal person I've ever met. She's been indispensable to me during my recovery. "

"I heard. You look like you are doing very well."

"I am improving all the time. Some days are better than others."

Velvet covered arching couches and stuffed chairs, their padding tacked down with button latches, filled the room.

Mr. Davis rolled over to a walnut sideboard. Crystal decanters covered the glossy surface.

"Would you care for a drink?"

She was taken aback and resisted the urge to look at her watch. Wasn't it only eleven? "No, thank you."

"What was I thinking?" He smiled and rolled toward the couch. With a firm movement, he gestured for her to sit down. "My sleeping schedule has been quite off. I occasionally get the times mixed up."

"Oh, that's awful. I understand." She perched on the edge of the stiff sofa and glanced around.

The painted flowers extended into a full fresco that spread out across the far wall. A naked woman stood beside a waterfall. Her sad face stared down at a young man bleeding at her feet.

"Wow, that's intriguing," she said.

He stared at her, ignoring the art even as he answered. "Persophone and Cupid."

"I don't remember the story quite like that."

"Call it a fanciful interpretation....Perhaps my own interpretation. So...." He tipped his head back and continued to study her. His eyes glittered behind the wire-rimmed glasses. "You are here about the flowers."

"Well, yes." Elise felt a flicker of surprise. "How did you know?"

He chuckled softly. "This is a small town. Hard to keep little whisperings quiet in a small town."

"I was just curious. Especially after...." She pressed her lips together, unsure of how to continue.

"After the death of my son and the lawsuit?'

Elise nodded.

"Why, we all need to forgive in order to move forward, like the bible says, right? After all, death will rise to greet us all most unexpectedly one day." He laughed again, sounding cold. Elise felt goosebumps rise on her arms.

She rubbed at them self-consciously. "I'm not sure everyone would be able to forgive in this case. I mean," she cleared her throat, "rumor has it the brakes were sabotaged?"

He shook his head. "Couldn't be proven. You should know better and investigate these things before you burst in with questions. All in all, our fine Angel Lake police force concluded that it was probably a rat chewing through the cables to make a nest for winter." He looked at her again, this time, his eyes hidden as the glasses reflected the window behind her. "We know how those rats are."

"So, you're saying you didn't have a problem with Cameron? After the loss of your son?"

"I'm saying that after my accident, I had to either move forward or let myself die. I was tempted to die. I'll admit. My niece gave me a reason to move forward. She's an orphan you know." He turned his head, and the reflection disappeared. His eyes were dark and sorrowful. "And I was still grieving my son. We needed each other, I think."

Elise nodded.

"As for the flowers, well I sent twenty-nine of them." He clapped his hands together. "And if you are as smart as you think you are, I'm sure you'll figure out why."

"Why the Delphinium?"

"Ah," he nodded. "That shouldn't be too hard to figure out either. Now, it's time for you to go. Let me show you the way out." He rolled to the door. As he turned to see if she was following, something small hit the floor and rattled away. A prescription bottle. For the first time, he looked flustered as he pushed the chair after the bottle.

It rolled to Elise's feet, and she scooped it up. Spinning it slightly, she tried to read the bottle, even as she handed it back. He snatched it from her hand and transferred it beneath the lap blanket.

Elise smiled and twisted the door handle. The heavy carved door opened easily on smooth hinges and allowed a rectangle of sunshine to fall upon the green marble. "One more thing," she said as she stepped out. "Where were you on the day of the 27th?"

"I was with my niece doing physical therapy in Tallahassee. I have the receipt from the hotel we stayed at. Be careful, Elise. You're playing with the big kids now." Once again, he planted a confident grin across his face and closed the door.

21

After her visit with Mr. Davis, Elise pulled into the RiteAid parking lot. This business housed a pharmacy, along with every odd-and-end item from hair care products, toys, to seasonal items. There was even a cooler in the back to pick up milk.

A few minutes later, Brad knocked on her car window. She jerked in surprise before opening the door. "You're always scaring me."

"Such an easy target. And, fancy meeting you here."

Elise laughed. "I read your mind. Or your text."

"Sorry I'm late," he said. Sweat trickled down his brow. "Turns out the jog was a bit farther than I expected from the courthouse."

Elise's ears perked up. Jogging? Potential jogging partner maybe? Her gaze fell to his muscular legs under long shorts, and then up to his rippled abs exposed as he used the bottom of his shirt to wipe his face. Her mouth went dry.

"Right?" His voice startled her, and she glanced up meeting his eyes crinkled with amusement.

"It is pretty far," she murmured back.

"I just can't let you think I can't keep up with you. Speaking of that, when were you going to tell me you went to Mr. Davis's?" He raised an eyebrow.

She felt the heat flood her face and decided that changing the subject was the best course of action. "Has Mrs. McMahon ever been considered a suspect?"

"At this point, everyone near Cameron is considered a suspect until we can rule them out."

"So, has she been ruled out yet?"

He grinned mischievously. "So far, only I've been ruled out. And you are still one of my top contenders."

"That's not even funny."

"What can I say? I think you might look pretty cute in handcuffs."

She gave him a punch in the arm. "Start with that."

"Yeah, assaulting an officer. I know there were some earlier ones…. Oh yeah, messing with witnesses."

"Oh, brother." Elise smiled and glanced down at her Fitbit. She stifled a groan. Two thousand more steps needed today.

"Let me think of what else. Tampering with an investigation. Illegal parking. You're just racking up crimes." He gestured to where her car sat outside the convenience store.

"That's not illegal."

"Customers only." He mimicked the owner and pointed to the sign that stood tilted after a previous customer backed into it.

"All right, all right, I'll move my car. I need to get to Lavina's anyway." She tipped her head. "After we talk to Sylvia of course."

"We?" he asked, fanning the front of his t-shirt to cool himself off.

"You. I mean you. Now can we go?"

He tipped his head like he was considering it. Flipping her hair off her shoulder, she ignored him and walked into the convenience store.

Sylvia was at the cash register, looking harried and very pregnant. Her face was flushed, and her blonde hair plastered back in a sweaty ponytail.

"Can I help you?" she asked as they came in.

Brad walked over to the register. "Hi, Sylvia. I'm Brad Carter from Angel Lake PD. Do you think you have a few minutes to talk to us?"

She licked her chapped lips and glanced in the far corner where the pharmacy was located. The pharmacist stared sternly at them before tapping his wrist and holding up five fingers.

"Yeah, I guess I have a few minutes." She lumbered from behind the counter, looking even bigger than just a few days earlier when Elise had seen her. They followed her to the back of the building. "Break room's in there." She gestured and walked over to the fan blowing in the corner. The fan's dirty blades made a whirring noise as she tipped her head and held the collar of her shirt open in front of it.

An old Coke machine stood against the wall. Brad jangled some coins in his pocket. "Want a drink?" he offered Sylvia.

She looked at him dully before nodding.

He inserted the coins. "What would you like?" She shrugged, uninterested.

"Right." He nodded and pressed the keys. A bottle of water popped out below with a clunk against the clear door. Twisting the lid, he handed it over to her. "So, we've been asking a few questions about your whereabouts on the afternoon of the 27th."

"I heard," she said in the same tired voice.

"Yeah. Well, there's something kind of weird going on with the dental appointment you said you were at on that day. Mind telling us what happened, in your words?"

She closed her eyes and took a long chug of the water, the plastic bottle crinkling as it emptied. It seemed to refresh her because her blue eyes were brighter when she opened them. "I made the appointment at noon. I know this because I timed it so I could go during my lunch break. At my old job. Before I got fired." She slumped against the wall as the last few words seemed to drain her again.

"And...?" Brad prompted. He pulled out a chair at the break room table.

"And, when I came in they said, 'No, you made this appointment at 11:15. Only there's no way I would have made it at that time. It was a Thursday. That was payroll day. I had to make it at noon because Cameron wouldn't let me take time off earlier than that."

Brad nodded. "Any idea why they had the wrong time?"

She shook her head. "But I have proof I made it at noon."

"Really?" Brad sat straighter in his chair. "What proof is that?"

"I went home and found the card. It was in with the rest of my stuff jammed in plastic bags. Out in the front yard."

"Your stuff was sitting in the yard in plastic bags?" Elise couldn't help herself. Brad shook his head warningly.

"Yeah. That was the day Frank kicked me out." She put her hand on her belly. "He said he wasn't taking care of no drug dealer's baby and to get out."

"Drug dealer? Isn't it Cameron's baby?" Again the words came out before Elise realized. This time, Brad cleared his throat.

"Yeah, it's Cameron's. Frank always called him that." Sylvia looked up at the clock and then back at Brad. "Look, I need to be getting back to work. Is there anything else?"

"Just one more thing. Were you on your two weeks notice at that time?"

She sighed. "Yeah. Good ol' Cameron was feeling generous and said I could finish out the month before he let me go." Her eyes darted to Elise. "He was being very sweet."

Elise felt the rebuke for her earlier attempts at encouragement. She nodded.

"Now, if there isn't anything else, I need to go before I lose this job, too."

"No, there's nothing more right now. Thank you for your time." Brad smiled. "By the way, when are you due?"

"Two more months." She groaned and grabbed her back. "And he is a kicker."

"He?"

"Yeah, a boy. Cameron's first son."

"Do you know if Cameron had any other kids?"

"Nope, not that I knew of. Until the letter came out about your friend." She nodded towards Elise. "I guess that lady knew she was his daughter. Probably thought she was going to get all that money without having to share. But I guess heir number two put a kink in that plan."

Sylvia grimaced and clutched at her back. "Look, I know you want to figure out who killed Cameron. But, all I wish is that things could go back to the way they once were. Before I made that horrible mistake. My marriage wasn't perfect, but Frank and I... we had good times. That's all gone now." Her eyes welled up and she angrily wiped at them. "Can I go now?"

When Brad nodded, she shuffled out of the break room and back to her station.

"Well, that's interesting," Brad mumbled, rubbing the back of his neck. They started for the door.

"What's interesting? You think Lavina cares that she's soon going to have a brother?"

"I think it's interesting that your friend was the only child heir of his estate until recently. And now the other competition for the inheritance is one of the main suspects." He shoved his hands in his pockets.

"Oh, come on, Brad. You know Lavina. Why in the world would she ever need money? She's totally a success in herself. She could have claimed to be his daughter at any time and reaped the rewards. But she didn't. She didn't want anyone to know."

"Exactly." They'd reached her car now.

Elise twiddled her keys. "Exactly what? Quit talking in riddles."

"She didn't want anyone to know. Pretty curious, don't you think?"

"No. I absolutely don't think it's curious that you don't want it known that your dad is the local scum lord of the town. If it were me, I'd keep it a secret too." She felt heat rise in her face at his insinuations.

"A secret that seems to have paid off in spades." He glanced at her and casually leaned against her car. "I'm just saying, Elise. Maybe you're too close to this."

"Brad. She is not the killer. Stop thinking about her that way. It's been horrible. Everyone's whispering that she poisoned him. I'm seriously worried about her having a breakdown. You have no idea how terrible this has been for her. Why hasn't everyone been going after Frank like this? He had the same motive."

"You're right about people being freaked about the poison. We're hearing rumblings of it from weird places. This town is about to combust. And, by the way, Frank and Lavina's motives are not exactly the same. There wasn't financial gain for Frank. In fact, it makes less sense for him to have done it because he kicked Sylvia out. If he wanted Cameron dead, you'd think he would have played nice with Sylvia since it was her child that stood to inherit all that money."

"He doesn't have the brains to think through details like that. Remember, Frank attacked Cameron in front of a bar, for crying out loud. And there was a gun involved!"

"You never know, Elise. People continue to astound me all the time." Brad glanced at her with a sad smile. "I know this isn't easy. But, at the end of the day, I have a job to do. And that's to bring some justice to whoever killed Cameron." He reached for her shoulder. "Even, if at the end, it's going to make you hate me."

"You're wrong, Brad, that's all I can say. I'll see you later." Her eyebrows rumpled in hurt and confusion. She climbed in her car with a brief wave out the window in his direction, before backing out and heading home.

22

Elise set her bowl of granola on the counter and pulled the laptop closer. She logged into Facebook and searched for Cameron McMahon.

He came up as the first person she might know. She clicked his profile and took a bite of cereal. Crunching, she scrolled through his pictures.

Max bumped her feet with his head. "I know, it makes me feel like a stalker too."

With a loud meow, Max stretched up on her leg. "Ow, ow, ow!" she yelled as his nails made their little pinpricks of annoyance at not being fed. She brushed him down and opened a can of food.

Then, she jumped back on the computer. The third picture in one of his folders made her pause. There was Cameron sprawled out on his boat, his normally greased back hair falling forward in a natural wave. At his feet was a little dachshund with a white star on his forehead.

"Herman," Elise whispered.

After a moment, she began searching the words "pet finder, missing dogs." Several animal shelters popped up. She pulled her bowl over and took bites as she scrolled through the pictures of dogs.

The shelters close to her had a few small dogs, but none that looked like Herman. On a whim, she searched the farthest shelter, nearly two hours away.

And there he was. Under a broad blue flag that said, "Adopt me."

* * *

"Lavina, will you come with me? To see if this dog is Herman?"

"Hush your mouth! You think you found him?"

"I'm hoping I did. It's a long shot but it seems too coincidental to ignore. I just hope he's still there. When I called the animal services, they weren't able to give me any information about him."

"Wait a minute. We're driving two hours on a hunch this might be the dog, and you don't even know if he's still there or not?"

"He was there as of last night because his picture was on the website as available."

Lavina had hesitated only a second before she answered, "Well, honey, I just need to find my scarf since we'll be taking my convertible. The top is definitely coming down! I'll see you in ten minutes to pick you up."

Despite herself, Elise laughed as she hung up. As usual, Lavina was always there for her.

* * *

Lavina pulled up as promised in her white Camaro. The horn honked twice to let Elise know she'd arrived. Quickly, Elise locked the door and ran out to the driveway. The top was indeed down, and Lavina glanced over at her with jeweled sunglasses that sparkled in the sunlight. "Come on, slow poke. We have a dog to rescue."

"You are the best!" Elise clambered into the seat, wincing slightly at the heat of the leather against her bare legs under her shorts. She looked over at her friend, dressed to the nines in a pink fitted dress.

Lavina checked the knot of the blue scarf tied at the base of her neck to make sure her hair was secure. "Honey, you ready for an adventure?"

"Let's go!"

Stomping on the gas, Lavina chirped all four tires leaving black marks in the driveway.

"Lavina! Be careful!"

"Relax! Don't be such a control freak."

"I don't think...."

"Elise, you don't even like being a passenger in a car. I've seen you stomp the imaginary brakes at an intersection. We're in a Camaro." She smiled, flashing white teeth. "That's the way you do it." Without waiting for a response, she reached for the volume to blast Adele's newest CD.

Elise leaned back in the seat and watched the trees flash green overhead. She closed her eyes and breathed deeply. Such a beautiful day.

Two hours later, they pulled up to the town of Northgate's animal shelter. "Here we go," Lavina said, grabbing her white purse. She shut the door and minced in her Louboutins up the front steps of the building, belying the way the car had squealed into the parking lot.

Fluorescent bulbs brilliantly lit the inside. A woman at the counter looked up from her book as they entered.

Elise wrinkled her nose. A strong stench of animal urine permeated even the front room. From the back came an insistent bark that reverberated over and over, punctuated by soft yips.

Sorrow wash over her.

Next to her, Lavina gave her a small nudge towards the counter.

"Can I help you?" the woman asked. Her hair was threaded with silver and pulled severely back into a ponytail at the base of her neck.

"Hello. I called about a dog earlier today."

The lady's lips quirked into an ironic grin. "We get a lot of phone calls about dogs."

"Oh, yes." Elise shook her head, slightly embarrassed. "It was a male dachshund. He was a little older, brown, with a white patch right about here." Elise pointed to her forehead.

"Oh, yes. Actually, we did have one matching that description, but he's gone now."

Her heart sank. "Is he…."

"Oh, sugar. No. This is a no-kill shelter. We have a very high adoptive rate here, and we are rather proud of our record. And, with him being a pure breed. Well, that's everyone's first choice. We don't keep those kinds of dogs long around here. He left just yesterday."

Elise's chest burned with disappointment. So close.

The woman opened a drawer and rifled through folders. She smiled wryly up at them. "Our system is pretty archaic. Let me see if I can find where he was sent. I have a feeling…." She pulled out a folder and flopped it open on the counter. Licking her fingers, she flicked through the papers then stopped to study one before peeling it from the pile. "Yes, it's like I thought. He did leave yesterday. Went to the dachshund rescue." She slid the paper across the counter to them. "This look like your dog?"

Elise studied the paper and the tiny black and white photo of the dachshund. Her brow wrinkled. There was the white star. She glanced at the address. The rescue was in Fort Orchard, the next town over. "You think we could head over there and see him?"

"Let me call and find out." She picked up the phone and began dialing. With her hand over the mouthpiece, she continued, "There will be the standard fee if this dog does indeed turn out to be yours. Although he came in good health, we automatically immunize them. Oh. Hello?" Her voice raised as the call was answered. "I'm calling about that little dachshund you picked up yesterday. Yes, yes, that's him. I have the owners here looking for him."

Elise shifted uneasily at being referred to as the owner.

"You still have him? Oh? Really? Okay. Okay."

Each pause and okay felt like rocks tumbling in Elise's stomach. Did they or didn't they? Just clarify it one way or the other!

The woman hung up the phone. "Looks like you are in luck. They do indeed have him, and he's still with the main coordinator. They haven't fostered him out yet." She scribbled out an address. "Here you go. They're expecting you."

Back at the car, Elise sank into the passenger seat after a quick yelp of pain.

"Darlin', you must remember to bring a sweater."

"What am I going to do if this ends up not being the right dog after all? And why on earth would I want a sweater in this heat?"

"To shield the seat, of course." Lavina took the paper from Elise and studied it. Placing it in the center console, she said, "I have an idea. Let's get a bite to eat. My Grandma always said everything is clearer with food in your stomach."

* * *

At the restaurant, Lavina steeped a teabag while Elise tucked into a slice of apple pie.

Lavina lifted her cup for a sip. Unexpectedly, she wiped a tear trickling down her cheek. "I tell you, Elise. All of this is getting to me."

Elise's heart squeezed. "We'll figure this out, Vi."

"You don't get it. I had two clients cancel on me last week. I'm getting the side-eye at the deli. You know how rumors go. People think I did it."

Elise sighed. "I don't know why they wouldn't be supporting you."

"Right? Maybe if he died of a gunshot. But somehow the fact that he died by poison makes people...." Her voice dropped to a whisper, "I think people are scared of me!"

"Don't be silly, Vi."

"I'm serious! I saw Manny dump his coffee out after I gave him a mug. And when I walk out to the counter to take an order, I've been greeted by some anxious faces. No one wants me to handle their food."

"Are you sure you aren't just interpreting this all through some general anxiety of the investigation. I mean, this is all a lot to take in."

Lavina set the cup down on the counter and tapped her pink lacquered nail against the rim. She pursed her lips and looked out the window, her eyes focused on nothing. "Isn't it weird how time changes everything? Just one event and nothing is the same again."

"Don't worry. It's going to work out. They're going to catch the killer."

She batted heavily mascaraed eyelashes at Elise. "You have more confidence than I do in the efficiency of Angel Lake's police force."

"Brad seems to be doing okay."

"Brad."

"Lavina, please. We've known him since high school."

"He certainly impresses you more now than he did back then."

"I didn't talk much to any guy back then." Elise blushed. "Can you say wallflower? I was terrified of my own shadow."

Lavina snorted. "You were as much of a wallflower as I was shy and demure. You just lacked confidence is all. So, when did you last talk with Brad?"

Elise shifted. This conversation was rapidly treading into uncomfortable territory. "Last week. We ran into each other at the coffee shop."

Lavina arched an eyebrow, one she had to fill in after over-plucking. Elise never understood why Lavina would pluck her eyebrows only to redraw them on.

"What are you looking at me like that for?" Elise asked crossly.

"I just think it's interesting," Lavina drawled out.

"Well, interesting or not, let's get going."

* * *

That night both women were exhausted from the day driving around in the sun. But, at least one slept. Little Herman rested his starred head on Elise's lap all the way home. She didn't know yet how she was going to reintroduce the doxie back to Mrs. McMahon, but for now, she was content.

23

The next morning, Elise spent nearly an hour trying to locate Max, who was clearly unhappy with the newest intruder. She finally found him squeezed behind the couch and tried to coax him out with a piece of lunch meat. She lay on the floor with her arm outstretched. "Come on, baby. It's okay."

His eyes glowed at her, and his ears flattened back. He'd clearly not forgiven her for allowing Herman to snuggle in under the covers in her bed to sleep the night before.

"Okay, then." She pushed herself up and brushed her off hands. "You stay there and pout. He's just going to be here for a little while. Try and play nice."

In the kitchen, she filled a bowl with the dog food that had come home with them from the rescue. Herman happily dug into the food like a fat old bear in a honey pot. She gave him a scratch on his neck.

Looking at the time on her Fitbit, she realized she had to get out and walk the other dogs. She wasn't ready to bring Herman with her yet, still not quite sure of how to announce she'd found him. "You guys be good," she called from the door and thumbed up her jogging playlist.

Two hours later, Elise arrived home to an excited Herman springing from a pile of fluff that had once been her couch cushion. A piece of the cotton still remained trapped between his two front teeth.

Max stared angrily from atop of the china cabinet, tail lashing.

She covered her mouth with her hand to stifle a whimper. After a second to digest the situation, she squared her shoulders. "Right. Calling Brad, STAT."

She reached for the cell and nearly dropped it when it began to ring.

"Hello?"

"Elise! Are you free?" Lavina's voice over the phone was shrill with panic.

"What's going on?" The hair on the back of Elise's neck prickled at her friend's tone. She sunk onto the couch, inciting Max to jump down from the cabinet at the lap invitation. "You okay?"

"Can you come down here. Like right now?"

Lavina didn't need to use the code word. Elise could hear panic threaded through her voice. "On my way!" Elise stood, dumping the cat unceremoniously from her lap. Max meowed and stalked off to the corner to bathe his face. Herman bounced over to comfort his new friend, sending Max racing back to the top of the cabinet.

After freeing the dog from his cotton floss, Elise let him out into the backyard while she changed her clothes. After he returned inside, she darted a look around the living room and sighed. "I'll sort this all out later after I talk to Brad. Please be good," she begged.

* * *

Elise drove down the street toward Sweet Sandwiches, looking for an empty parking stall. Her mind spun with the crazy direction Lavina's life had taken recently. Every spot was taken except for a few tight ones near the ally. She pulled into one with a grimace, hating to parallel park.

The bell rang as Elise opened the door to the deli shop. The spicy scent of salami greeted her, and she couldn't help but inhale deeply.

Inside was crowded with people. She wiggled her way towards the back where she knew she'd find Lavina.

Her friend looked completely exhausted with her red hair shooting out like hayseeds from a scarecrow's hat around the silk bandana. She was nodding at an irate woman in front of her. Elise joggled up next to the customer.

The dark haired woman waved her hands in dramatic fashion. "But, Ms. Lavina, we were sick! It happened last week, right after we ate your sandwiches."

"I can assure you, Mrs. Burgen, we only use the finest meats here. Everything is refrigerated per regulation as required. Our business is up to every code and passes a yearly inspection. There is nothing here that would have caused your family to be sick."

"Oh, no, no, no. Ms. Lavina, please. We went on a picnic. Drove all day down to Flowing lake. And, I'm telling you, my poor Ralph threw up all afternoon. He had to sit in the passenger seat on the way home. With a bucket! And he hates to sit there. He hates my driving. But he was sick, so sick. Sick because of you." A knobby finger pointed under Lavina's eyes.

Her friend drew in a deep breath, then answered patiently. "Did you eat some of the sandwiches too?"

Ms. Burgen seemed reluctant to reply. "I don't like liverwurst. That was for him. I had the turkey."

"Last Saturday was 102 degrees outside. How long after you made the sandwiches did you eat them?"

Ms. Burgen opened and closed her mouth like a fish. Her curls shook as she squeezed her hands together in anger. Finally, she blurted, "Don't you turn this around on me, Missy! I'm not the poisoner here in this town! You! You did this!" She stomped one of her thick heels and spun around pushing the other customers out of her way as she rushed for the door.

"Well," Lavina swallowed and wiped her brow. "That was unpleasant."

"What was that all about?"

"You haven't heard?" Lavina's carefully painted eyebrows drew up. "My goodness. I clearly have the juicy gossip this time." She indicated the door as another customer came in and called to her employee. "David? Could you take care of them?" Then, back to Elise. "Let's go to my office, shall we?"

They maneuvered down the white hallway and into the small back room. There were employee table and chairs, a counter filled with coffee making items, a sink, and a microwave.

Lavina grabbed a chipped white mug and filled it with water. Her hands were trembling.

"Whats going on?" Elise asked, as a knot tightened in her stomach. She'd never seen her friend this upset before.

"Apparently, the toxicity report on Cameron is everyone's number one topic of discussion lately. Along with me being in the will." She set the cup in the microwave with a clatter and shut the door. "My lucky day." After punching in the time, she drooped into the metal chair with her forehead in her hands.

Elise closed her eyes. This changed everything. She dragged her attention back to her friend. "I'm sorry."

"And you thought I was exaggerating yesterday." She yanked the microwave door open before it dinged and retrieved the cup. Rifling through her teabags, she selected Easy Now and popped it in the water. "She hasn't been the only one. It's been unseasonably hot, and people aren't properly taking care of the food they're eating outside. Suddenly, people think I'm poisoning them." Her forehead wrinkled as she fought back tears. She swallowed a hiccup, shook her head, and smiled brightly. "I'm not going to do it. I'm not going to let them affect me."

"Oh, Lavina." Elise felt her heart squeeze with sympathy. "What are they thinking? They've known you forever!"

"What can I say, one minute they love you, and the next," she drew her finger across her throat. "Something about murder makes everyone jumpy."

"I'm with you. I have your back." Elise grabbed Lavina into a hug. "I won't let anyone be mean to you. They'll have to come through me first."

Lavina clung to her for a moment before pushing away. She dabbed under her eyes. "Great. Make me a sappy ol' mess while I'm trying to talk tough." She fished in her purse for a tiny mirror and flipped it open to inspect her makeup. Her mouth dropped open at the sight of her hair. In a well-practiced movement, she had the scarf off and hair smoothed before retying the scarf again. She peeked into the mirror again. This time satisfied, she slid the silver compact away and took a long drink of her tea. "Anyway. So that's how my day is going. Yours?"

"Well, I ran the 3k around the lake for the first time."

"Really? Congratulations." Lavina sipped again. "You're going for the half-marathon after all, eh?"

"I'm determined. I'm doing life differently now. And, the best part is, today, I came home to discover I get to redecorate."

Lavina smiled. "Sounds like a good story coming up."

"Want to guess?"

"After a day like this, don't make me guess."

Elise lifted a finger. "One word. Herman."

Her friend chuckled. "What are you going to do about him?"

"Well, after I leave here, assuming I don't have to take him to the vets for cushion overeating, I'm going to call Brad. Hopefully, we'll return him tonight."

"Brad," Lavina said in a light sing-song.

Elise shrugged, still bothered at how Brad had focused his investigation on Lavina. But she didn't want to tell her friend that and worry her. "Just friends. For a long time. In fact, the way this is going, I'll probably die a cat lady."

"I may deny you were a wallflower, but a cat lady, I can see that." She winced as Elise fake-punched her arm. "All these years, I called it right."

"Whatever. This cat lady is trying to save your butt."

Lavina smiled again before stretching her arms. She rubbed her face with her hands, sighed, then stood up. "Well, I guess I need to get to it. Thanks for being my back up."

"You bet. No one calls out my best friend." Elise's voice was filled with determination. "I mean no one."

24

Elise opened her door to a frowning Brad standing in full police gear with a dog kennel balanced against his hip.

"Hi." She smiled. Max scurried over, fatter now, and did his characteristic body-stretch on Brad's leg. Brad's eyes widened at the sting of Max' claws. "Oh. You naughty cat! Shoo!" Max slinked off with satisfaction, his tail curled in the air like a question mark.

"Where's the dog?" he said in a monotone.

"He's over there." She pointed to a pile of blankets in the corner of the room. A dark muzzle poked out from the center, nostrils flaring at the newcomer.

Brad walked in, his leathers squeaking, and squatted down. He held out his hand. The muzzle grew into a little face with liquid brown eyes staring up. "Hey, little guy. You're okay." Slowly, Herman emerged from his bed. His tail wagged as Brad petted him.

"So." Brad looked up from the dog, his eyebrow arched. He began his patented —I'm not saying anything — interrogation style.

The silence grew between them. Finally, Elise cleared her voice and began. "It's like I said. I've just been so curious about where this dog disappeared to. I spent some time searching on google, and boom! Up he popped."

"Up he popped, huh?" He lifted his chin as Herman tried to lick his face. "And no thought to calling me? Your ol' buddy? An actual detective?"

Elise shrugged and tossed a half-smile in his direction. "We weren't sure it was him until we drove down there."

"Who?"

"Lavina and I."

"She thinks she's a detective. Doesn't she, Herman?" This time, the dog got a few excited licks in. "But she's going to get her butt in trouble. Mmhmmm." He stood with the dog in his arms. "So, you ready to return him?"

Elise nodded. "Like yesterday. And, I wasn't trying to do this behind your back. It just happened to work out that way."

Brad snorted as he placed the dog in the kennel and carefully hefted it. "Okay. Let's go, you little trouble maker."

* * *

Ten minutes later, they pulled up outside the McMahon's house. Manicured bushes hedged in the stately front portico. Elise could scarcely see the front entryway as it was blocked with people; housekeepers, gardeners, and personal drivers. Several of them clapped when Brad lifted the plastic carrier out. Elise was taken aback by the happiness on their faces.

"They've truly missed this dog," she whispered over to Brad.

In the back of the crowd hovered Mrs. McMahon. She wore no makeup, and her face was drawn from grieving. She took a few uncertain steps forward to meet them. "You've found our Herman?"

Brad placed the kennel down at the base of the steps. Everyone leaned to look in. "I believe so." He fiddled with the latch for a moment and opened the carrier.

Cautiously, the little dachshund peeked out. At the sight of the star on his forehead, several of the workers cried out, "Herman! Oh, Herman!" The dog sprang forward at their voices, his tail wagging ferociously. He leaped from the outstretched arms of one person to another, licking faces and barking excitedly.

"Awww." Elise smiled, feeling happy warmth in her chest.

"Good job, Detective." Brad grabbed her around the shoulders in a one-armed hug.

Mrs. McMahon wobbled down the stairs in her house slippers. She bent down and reached a hand towards the little dog. "Herman?"

His response was instantaneous. The hair rose on his back as a low growl rose from his throat. Mrs.

McMahon's eyebrows raised as she stepped back. Loud barks erupted from Herman as he pranced back and forth before her.

The crowd of people reacted with stunned silence. Finally, the gardener scooped up the angry dog. "Shh," he scolded. "Why are you barking at the lady like that? You're okay. You're home now."

The dog settled down in his arms. The gardener shot a look at Mrs. McMahon. "I'm sorry about that. Must be upset about the Mister."

She nodded and made a small dismissive movement with her hand. "Keep him with you today, Jerry. Maybe that will help."

The gardener nodded and hugged the dachshund close. "I sure did miss you, little man." That seemed to release the other workers who gathered back around him to pet Herman.

Brad was silent as he watched. Mrs. McMahon raised her hand in goodbye before she slowly and painfully went back into her house. The rest of the house staff filed in behind her.

"You ready?" he asked Elise. She nodded and returned to the car.

"Do you think that was odd?" Elise buckled the seatbelt.

"More than odd." Brad's mouth was tight as he looked over his shoulder to back up.

Elise thought for a minute. Something someone had told her once about Herman....

"You okay if I make a stop on the way home?" Brad interrupted her thoughts. She nodded.

After fifteen minutes of driving, Brad turned down Old Farm Road. Yellow scotch broom growing on the side of the road swayed like hula dancers in the car's passing breeze.

Elise looked at the run-down houses and then back to Brad. "Where are we going?"

"Thought I might check in with my friend, Frank. It's been a while since I've talked with him."

"With me with you? You really going to do this?" Elise asked.

He pulled into the driveway and yanked the emergency brake. "We're here, aren't we? Just do me a favor and be like a broken headset."

"What does that mean?"

"Silent."

Elise rolled her eyes and climbed out of the car. Together, they walked up the driveway.

The house was in serious disarray. Gray paint peeled from the siding in flakes. Shrubbery in desperate need of water sagged against the house. Elise felt a flicker of panic when the porch groaned under their weight and carefully avoided the rotting boards.

Brad knocked on the door firmly. A calico cat skittered from behind a bush and ran hell-bent at the noise.

The face meeting them on the other side of the screen door was anything but friendly.

"What do you want, Brad?"

Elise looked up at Brad nervously. He didn't flinch at Frank's tone. If anything, he seemed even more self-assured than just a moment earlier.

"Nothing big. Just some standard questions we've been asking a few people in your neighborhood."

Frank opened the door an inch, and Brad linked his fingers in the crack. He opened it all the way as Frank took a few steps back.

"You going to make this quick? I've got to get to the gym." Frank didn't seem to notice he was clad in tight jeans and bare feet.

Elise glanced around but there was no gym bag in sight. Her eyes narrowed. She worked hard to mask her look of disbelief.

Brad's features relaxed into an easy smile."This won't take long."

Frank led them back to a dirty kitchen. Elise shrank into herself, afraid to touch anything. Gingerly, she sat in one of the plastic covered chairs at the table with the men.

Brad started. "So, I heard you had a violent run-in with Cameron?"

Frank's face stiffened with anger. "That was years ago. He reached for his gun, and I reacted. It was just a split second, or I would have been dead." Frank pinched the bridge of his nose. He stared at Elise and Brad. "You hear me? I had my chance to kill him. If I wanted him dead, he'd be gone."

"He was the one with the gun? We're just trying to sort things out here." Brad's voice was low and even.

"Yeah. Him. What, you heard it was me? You think I look like the kind of guy who'd have a gun?"

Brad didn't say anything. His gift was in his pauses, which usually prompted the other person to fill in the space.

"Look, Cameron was a waste of space. Anybody will tell you that. I hated him as much as the next guy. He knocked up my ol' lady! Still, I didn't kill him. There ain't a better man to make acquaintances with ol'Nick though." Frank cracked his knuckles which subconsciously emphasized his last thought.

Elise dearly wanted to ask Frank where he was when he left the movie theater. Under the table Brad's knee softly bumped into her leg, warning her to be still.

Swallowing hard, she controlled the urge to reach across the table and squeeze Frank's throat. Her gaze cut sidewise to Brad. Probably not a good idea in front of a cop. She'd get thrown in jail along with Vi, and then where would they be?

They'd be trading tater tots and eating crappy food off a plastic tray, that's where. And in the meantime, Cameron's killer would still be on the loose.

This whole thing seemed kind of unfair in the long run.

Brad laced his fingers on the table before him and leaned forward in a relaxed stance. Frank glanced at him before rolling his own shoulders. "I don't know why you're questioning me. I'd say this is harassment. I already had to give my whereabouts."

Brad nodded.

Frank reached for an empty can of coke in front of him and began tinkering with it, denting the sides of the can. "I was at the movies. I gave y'all my ticket stub. The popcorn kid saw me. I know because y'all questioned him already."

Brad nodded again.

The can snapped on the table as the dent popped out. Elise jumped.

"Are you guys done? I don't have anything else to say."

"Yeah, I think we're just about done here." Brad smiled disarmingly. He stood up and nodded at Elise. "You ready?"

A small sound of dismay shot out of Elise before she nodded. Slowly, she grabbed her purse.

Brad tucked the chair back under the table. It's wooden legs screeched on the linoleum. He gave the back of the chair a rat-a-tat-tat with a slap of his hands. "Just one final question."

Frank exhaled heavily.

"Why'd you change your wife's dental appointment?"

Frank laughed, revealing silver covering one of his canines. "What? Now I'm some kind of secretary? Why would I do that?"

Brad smiled. "You tell me."

"I didn't mess with her appointment, dude. You're barking up the wrong tree. That two-timing chick just bit off more than she could chew. You need to be going after her. Hell. He fired her just the day before. She was the love of my life, but I kicked her out. I don't have time to be worrying about her precious teeth."

"How were you so certain it wasn't your baby?" Elise interjected. Brad squeezed her shoulder.

"Army injury, little lady. Can't have no kids of my own." The tooth flashed at her again. "Course, everything else works a-ok, if you want to test it out." He gave her a wink.

"We'll be back to talk with you again, Frank. Don't be making any trips out of town without letting someone know." Brad gently led Elise out of the kitchen.

Frank followed them outside and leaned against the front doorway. His white tank top hung loosely around his skinny frame. "Y'all come back anytime, ya hear." He hawked up a wad of spit into the bushes behind them and slammed the door.

"Well, that was pleasant," Elise said as she slid into the front seat of the car.

"He's quite the character, that's for sure. Had a few stints in and out of jail but yet to do anything too terrible to send him to prison. Yet." Brad turned the ignition and backed out onto the street.

"He does have a point," Elise continued. "What good would it be to make an earlier dental appointment?"

"Puts her at the scene of the crime with no alibi. And with plenty of motive."

"So you think he framed her?"

"Either that or she's lying and knocked Cameron off herself. All I know is something's up with those two. But no one's out-smarted me yet."

25

"Oh, Lawd. You hear about the town meeting?" Lavina's voice quaked as it came through the cell phone.

"Lavina, you keep calling me and I won't know what to think the next time you text again."

"I don't have time to wait for you to answer a text. My life is in shambles right now." She groaned loudly. "It's about the poisoning. They're probably having this meeting to form a posse to come get me."

"What's going on?" Elise thought back to how Brad said there were rumblings in town. "Are you going?"

"Darlin', I do not stoop to answer gossip. They'll just have to have their little meeting without me." She paused for a second, and then urged, "But you should go."

"Me?"

"I need eyes and ears there, don't I? Who else am I going to get to do it besides my favorite cat lady? I know how you like to investigate stuff. I'm just thinking of you."

"Right." Elise agreed, rolling her eyes. "That's so thoughtful of you."

* * *

So that's how Elise found herself in the third row of a very tightly packed town meeting. Next to her sat the owner of the local garage. To the right was Mabel from the gym.

Mabel waggled her gray eyebrows and leaned over conspiratorially. "Did I not tell you? I knew that man didn't off himself. But now we're in a pickle. Have to deal with a poisoner."

The room was already overheated, with more bodies packing in by the minute. Elise fumbled through her purse for her checkbook and fanned it over her face. She nodded in agreement with Mabel, but inside she felt miserable. Was this really going to be about Vi?

The stout, older police captain meandered slowly to the podium. He grimaced as though his knees hurt, and rifled through a stack of papers that he eventually laid out on the stand. "All right, everyone. I'm calling this town meeting to order." He looked out at the crowd. "Quiet, everyone. It's hotter than two goats in a pepper patch in here, so let me get through this. Then we can vet your questions." He cleared his throat. "I just want to assure everyone we have all of our best men at the department on this case."

A man yelled from across the room. "Why are you playing around? It was poison. You have a motive. Why don't you go after him?"

Police Captain Stanley looked out into the room. "We are doing this by the law, one step at a time."

Someone else chimed in. "I saw that exterminator down by the town's well. Do you really think it's safe to let a suspect work near our water?"

Cries of outrage rang out around the room.

"Mr. Nichols has not been arrested for any crime. We are doing our investigation in an orderly manner. Y'all have to be patient."

One old man stood up, his cheeks dusky red from the exertion. Sweat popped out on his face as he made his way to the microphone. "Seems to me y'all are doing a lot of talking, and not a lot of action. Since last week, my water's been running green!"

"The water has been tested safe."

"For how long? Why should we believe you? How do we know when it's not safe? Just wait for someone else to keel over?"

The crowd grew rowdier. Stanley looked around for a gavel before resorting to pounding his fist on the podium. "All right! That's enough."

One little girl began crying. From the back of the room, a fight broke out. Two farmers argued. Five more people surged forward toward the microphone.

"I said that's enough! Everyone sit back down." This time, the Captain's sharply barked words grabbed the attention of the crowd. There was grumbling, but it faded as people began to find their seats.

Captain Stanley's dark eyes scowled under bushy eyebrows like bats peeping from a cave. Turning his head slowly, he surveyed the room. "We understand your concern. We're going to keep you safe."

"Like you kept Cameron safe?"

There were a few shouts of agreement and some snickers, but the voices settled back down.

The Captain focused on the old man. "And Albert, you can't be blaming your green water on anything but your own corroded copper pipes. It's a miracle your place is even standing."

There were a few soft chuckles among the crowd. Everyone around Angel Lake knew Albert's place. He was a man who always looked for a good deal, and he'd scored on a half acre out by the marsh years ago. He'd built a house there, despite everyone advising against it, and brought home a skinny wife. Together, they'd raised four boys up in it.

Those boys were known to be wild. Half the time they were hanging from the rafters. When the windows broke, Albert had simply taped over them with cardboard.

Now, his house was gradually sliding downhill as the porch pushed it deeper into the Tennessee mud.

Albert scowled but relaxed back in his chair with his arms folded in front of his chest. His scowl deepened as his neighbor good-naturedly elbowed him. "You know that's truth!"

Captain Stanely continued. "Your kids are safe. Your families are safe. The water facility tests the water every morning, and they're keeping things secure. Y'all don't need to be worrying about any of that. Just let it be, and let us get our jobs done."

"Now, are there any other questions? Besides the water?" this last remark was shot towards Mr. McGregor, the barber who had just shaken out his list.

"So you know for sure it was murder?"

"The toxicity reports show that the victim was indeed poisoned."

"What kind of poison?"

"We'll answer that at a later time."

"Do you know who did it?"

"We have a few suspects, and our detectives are diligently working on the case. The perpetrator will be caught." With that, he reshuffled the papers in front of him into something that resembled a stack. With a final smack on the podium, Captain Stanley ended with, "That's all we have for today. We will keep you informed. In the meantime, be good to each other and quit the damn vigilante mentality. We've got enough on our plate without busting up a bunch of yahoos."

He stepped down, and the town's secretary walked to the podium. In a soft voice, she closed with, "Okay, folks. Be sure y'all leave in an orderly fashion. I heard Grandma Babe has some new pies out."

People slowly filed out. Elise felt a tap on her shoulder and looked up to see Brad.

"Can you believe this?" she asked Brad.

"This is what happens when there is a murder in a small town. No one has nothing else to talk about. Makes investigating kind of hard because everyone is involved in the gossip circle. I never know if what I'm hearing is what they really think, or what Sally down the road told them over barbecue last night." He rubbed his chin, now clean shaven.

"You're going to figure this out. I know you will."

"If the Captain will give me some more wiggle room. He might not say it, but he's about locked his prime suspect down. He nearly has the arrest warrant signed already."

"Tell me it's Frank. He doesn't have an alibi, and he sure has a reason," Elise was just relieved that no one at the meeting had mentioned Lavina.

"I told you how I felt about his motive. Something just doesn't feel right."

"Like what?"

"Like why would he'd be going through with the divorce? He doesn't have much money."

"Maybe, you should look to see if he's come into any recently."

"You must think I'm an idiot. I've already raked through his financial records. Something's off about his motive."

"I can't explain why he does what he does, but I know he hated Cameron, and that kind of anger can make a person do crazy things. And he did have access to the poison."

"Yeah, he did. Which does make him the perfect suspect." Brad turned piercing dark eyes at her. "Or the perfect Patsy."

26

"I'm just feeling like Ms. Popularity, lately," Elise mumbled to herself. Two hours ago she'd received a phone call from Crystal, asking if she would be free later in the day for a glass of sweet tea. Highly suspicious, Elise had accepted solely on account of a tinge of humbleness she'd detected in Crystal's voice.

Now, with her little Toyota parked next to a Land Rover and Porshe, Elise felt slightly humbled herself. After applying a fresh application of lipstick, she fluffed out her hair. Quickly, she checked her eye makeup in the mirror, telling herself, "Let's just see what she has to say. And I love a good glass of sweet tea."

She'd just made it up the front steps when the door swung open.

"I heard you pull up. I'm so glad you were able to come over." Crystal's face looked gaunt, and her clothing hung on her frame. Elise felt a zing of shock and swallowed hard to avoid reacting.

"Come in. Come in." Crystal darted a look outside the door as if someone might be following Elise, and then whirled inside, leaving Elise on the threshold.

Elise stepped behind her. The house was gorgeous and filled with southern charm. An oak parquet floor stretched out from the entrance, framed at the sides by two white staircases that curved to the second story where they eventually joined together with delicate railing. Above them, a cut glass chandelier glittered.

Crystal was already far ahead and about to disappear into the formal parlor. Lengthening her steps, Elise made a quick effort to catch up with her.

In the parlor, a glass pitcher was already set up on a table, its outside dewy with condensation. Two glasses sat next to it with rims adorned with lemon slices. Elise settled into a chair across from Crystal. She waited for Crystal to begin and finally prompted her. "So, what's going on? Everything okay?"

Crystal looked up and covered her mouth with a well-manicured hand, the long fuchsia nails identical to the color on her lips. Her brown eyes welled with tears. "Oh, Elise! It just isn't true!"

Elise watched, flabbergasted.

Crystal hunched forward with her shoulders shaking.

"There, there," Elise leaned over to pat her arm. "It's okay. It's going to be okay."

"He's not a murderer!" Crystal blurted.

Elise sucked in her breath. "Who are you talking about?"

"Eric!" The word trailed out into a long sob. "My baby!"

At Crystal's words, Elise leaned back, blinking. "What's going on? Why are you saying this?"

"Officer Carter. He's been around here asking questions. He wants to know where my baby was the day that evil man died."

Elise nodded. "I'm sure it's just standard questioning. He's asked just about everyone in town that same question. After all, Cameron had a lot of enemies." She smiled weakly to lighten the mood.

Crystal's face flushed with anger as she looked up. "You think this is funny? This is my baby's life!"

Seeing the intensity of her emotion, Elise lowered her voice to a more soothing tone. "What is it you want from me?"

"I wanted to know—wasn't it, wasn't that the day you and Eric got together?"

Once again, Elise was stunned.

"Remember?" Crystal's anger quickly dissipated into a confident smile. "You know when you were looking for a car."

"I bought my car long before Cameron's murder, Crystal."

"Didn't you buy it out here? I'm sure there was more paperwork to sign."

Elise shook her head in confusion.

"Oh, come now. I'm just asking you, to maybe remember. Remember meeting Eric. At your house, I think? He was there with papers for you to sign?"

A cold wave washed down Elise's back as she finally understood Crystal's intentions. "You want me to lie for him?"

"No. Not lie." Crystal brushed the front of her blouse before raising her gaze to Elise. "I'm just asking you to think back on that day. And there is quite a financial incentive if you can recall it."

Elise was already waving her hand in the negative before the words were completely out of Crystal's mouth. "Absolutely not. What are you saying?"

Crystal pressed her lips together, turning them into two white lines. "Just think about it. Please. I believe that, in the end, it would be in everyone's best interests."

"Everyone's best interests?" She froze, remembering that Lavina had said she'd seen him at the dealership.

Crystal sniffled and pressed the knuckles of her hand against her mouth.

"Why do you want me to do this? Where was he when Cameron was murdered?"

"You promise not to tell. Tell me that you promise. No one will understand." Crystal stood up and walked stiffly to the window. She pulled a lace-trimmed handkerchief from her pocket and blotted her nose. "Everyone's going to know. Everyone's going to think he did it."

"Know what? Just tell me. I can't help you without knowing what's going on."

"He was with Mrs. McMahon," Crystal whispered. "She picked him up from his work. But if you tell anyone I'll deny it."

Elise tensed, realizing what Crystal was saying. Fear trickled in. Was her life in danger if Eric found out that she knew he had been there that day? She took a long swallow of her tea, trying to regain her composure.

"Oh, don't act so shocked. These December-May relationships happen all the time."

"It's not the age difference that's giving me pause, Crystal. Don't you think this is something that might help with the investigation?"

"No! The Angel Lake police are about as effective at their job as a mime with no hands. They just want to solve the case and close the book on it. They don't care who it is." She sniffled again and used the hanky to wipe her eyes. "They'll frame my baby! Those two couldn't help it if they fell in love. Anyone could see that the McMahon marriage was destined for divorce. Besides, the police already know who the killer is. Either that baby mama or her nasty husband. I have no idea why they're delaying the arrest of them."

"Oh, you can't seriously think that poor girl had anything to do with Cameron's death. What, she's going to drug him and drag him into the car? She's an itty bitty thing, besides being pregnant."

"You're standing up for that little piece of trash?" Crystal's face turned white. The botox had frozen any possible physical expression, but anger laced throughout her voice. Her eyes grew wider and wider.

Elise took a step back. What in the world? "She's not a piece of trash. She's a young girl who works hard, made a mistake, and recently found herself pregnant. And she's alone, very alone."

Crystal's hand gripping the glass shook as her knuckles whitened. "She is a whore. A low-class home wrecker who deserves what she got."

"Who's home did she wreck? Your own? What really bothers you about her?"

"I just think it's too convenient that her illegitimate son is suddenly the heir to Cameron's estate. It's uncouth."

Elise stood up. "As nice as this has been, I really need to get running."

As she was leaving, a display of white flowers on the sideboard caught her eye. Casually, she walked over. She grabbed a bloom and let the delphinium petals sift between her fingers, her brow wrinkling.

Crystal's heels clattered after her. "Weren't you listening to me?" Crystal continued. "You understand that Eric couldn't possibly have done it. He was with

Mrs. McMahon all afternoon. I'm sure her staff would attest to it."

"Where did you get these?" Elise asked, cutting her off.

"What?"

"These flowers. Where did you get them?"

"Oh." Crystal's pursed her pink slathered lips. "Those are from my beau." She fluttered her eyes coyly. "He brings them every Saturday."

Busy woman. Barely divorced and already a beau, Elise thought. Along with panting after Cameron. "What I meant is, where did they come from?"

"You mean the flower shop? Just that local one in town. Tamara's flowers, or whatever the yahoo."

"They are indeed beautiful. Again, thank you for the tea. I'm sure it will all work out for Eric."

"You do know that she brought your name up."

Elise shivered at the way Crystal's voice curled at the end of the sentence. "Who did?"

Crystal smiled as she looked at her. "The baby mama." She narrowed her eyes. "You didn't know?"

"What did she say?"

"She said that your friend, Lavina, got into some trouble, and you're really here on account of your bigwig husband about to bail your friend out. Conflict of interests maybe?"

"Oh, Crystal." Elise snorted and held up her bare ring finger for viewing. "Trust me, I'm not here to bail anyone but my own self out."

"I think you're being modest. Because I also heard that Eric has a little secret on your snotty friend. You know how this works, don't you? If you don't do this for me, I will ruin her. I'll do it without blinking an eye." She smiled again, a picture of a gentile woman. "Well. It really was a nice tea. Us divorcees need to stick together to defend against all that ugly gossip. I can be a real good friend. To both you and Lavina." She opened the front door. "Goodbye, dear. You just think about what I said. I'll expect to hear from you soon."

27

Elise drove around aimlessly for nearly an hour after her meeting with Crystal. Instead of getting clearer, the murder case was getting murkier despite all her intentions.

She glanced down by chance and saw her gas needle hovering nearly at "E." Feeling like the weight of the world was crashing on her, she pulled her car over to park.

"I can't hardly do this anymore." Elise whispered with her fingers pressed against her temples. "Dear God, just make it stop."

She looked out the windshield with a sarcastic laugh. There was no escaping it. Completely on autopilot, she'd driven herself to the lake.

"The place where this all began."

She got out of the car and stretched her legs. Almost half-heartedly, she checked her Fitbit. 3289 steps. Great. Not even a third of the way there for the day. She couldn't do anything about it now with her feet clad in the flimsy sandals she'd worn to tea. Jogging would have to wait.

Somehow, she wasn't even sorry about that.

As she walked under the trees, a breeze picked up the edge of her sundress. She held it down and breathed in the lake air deeply. If only it were that easy to wash away her anxiety.

A thicket of rushes whispered against each other and caught Elise's attention. The dark head of a duck bobbed as she rustled around rearranging her nest. Not wanting to disturb her, Elise crept away.

Why couldn't she figure out who had killed Cameron? Was it Frank? Eric? Mrs. McMahon? Was she going to be able to save Lavina?

Crystal's threat lurked inside her ear like the voice of a specter, eerie and sinister. She was going to ruin Lavina by outing her boyfriend if Elise didn't cooperate and say she'd been with Eric.

That woman made her skin crawl.

The wind picked up more, and she was blinded by her own hair. Her hands shook as she tried to scoop her hair back into a ponytail.

She felt like a failure.

Tears pricked her eyes. She couldn't take another minute of this. The meeting at Crystal's had to be exposed, come what may. Finding her cell, she scrolled for Brad's number with a lump in her throat. It was time to tell him everything she knew.

It was time to come clean.

"Hey, Elise," he answered, his voice low and sweet, making her smile even under the heavy feeling of discouragement. "Glad you called. I've got some stuff to share with you."

"Hi, Brad. I need to talk with you. You busy?"

There was just a hint of a pause. "You've never asked that before. What'd you do this time?"

"You go first." She walked under the trees, feeling slightly reinvigorated by the shade.

He laughed. "I hate to do it because I know whatever it is you want to tell me has gotta to be good. But here it is. I visited the Northgate animal shelter today. Actually, just got back."

"Seriously? And what did they say?" Reaching out, she began to play with a leaf growing from a low branch. Her finger traced the ridged underside.

"I was mostly curious about how they got that little dog. Luckily, their file on him was still open and they were happy to let me see it. On the 27th, a man dropped him off saying that he'd nearly hit the dachshund on the highway. But here's the funny thing. When I showed the assistant a few of the pictures I had with me, she identified the man right away."

"Brad! That was brilliant! Who was it?"

"You're going to love this. It's a fellow we both know by the name of Eric Bridgewell." He chuckled at Elise's gasp. "And there's more. The vet assistant had to run out in the parking lot to stop his car before he left. It seems they needed one more signature. She said Eric was most unhappy about being stopped, but he did sign the form. And the assistant got a good look at his passenger, describing her as an older, blonde woman."

"Who was it?"

"I was able to pull a picture off of Facebook to confirm it, and it was indeed her. Mrs. McMahon."

Elise sagged with relief against the tree. She didn't need to confess to Brad after all. "You really are so smart. I can't believe I ever doubted you."

"Me finding another suspect sure makes you sappy. Keep in mind, this is all still just circumstantial evidence. I still have my number one in mind."

"Who? Lavina? Oh, please. It could never be her. Be serious for a second. How much do you think he weighed? Over two hundred pounds? How do you suppose she lifted his weight and gotten him into the driver's side of the car? And where would she have gotten the poison?"

"Is that what's stumping you, Elise? Let me assure you that he was alive when he was in the car. He probably climbed in himself. There's no doubt he definitely knew whoever it was who killed him. As for the poison, we're still working on that."

She wrinkled her nose at hearing the smugness in his voice. "Well, now you're doing that conjecture thing you always accuse me of doing. How can you possibly know that?"

"His thigh had a purple injection site where the poison was administered. Probably knocked his heart out within minutes after he got it. Then, whoever it was, drove the Mercedes over the tracks and left it there. Cameron was slumped over so it wouldn't have been clear that he wasn't in the driver's seat. Sorry to tell you, but your friend absolutely would be capable of doing this."

"Quit saying that. She'd never do it."

"Just stating the facts, Ma'am."

Elise decided to change the subject. "Any more news about Frank?"

"I figured out where he was for those twenty minutes. Calling his parole officer. He has fifty hours of community service. Right now they're picking up garbage and fixing the white crosses on the highway. He's probably repainting the one at Flower's Cove right now."

"Flower's Cove?"

"Yeah. That's the other name they call the valley at Reicher cliff. Where Mr. Davis's son died. So, tell me. What were you calling about?"

"Aww. It's not a big deal now."

"Come on. Don't be like that."

"Well, I just have some theories on who I think did it myself. Just kind of spinning in my mind."

"Your spinning mind scares me. Let's go have lunch at Taco Del Santo. I have a feeling there's still something more you want to tell me."

"You don't have to ask me twice. I love that place."

"Oh yeah? Why?"

"Because. Tacos!"

28

At the restaurant, Elise waited to turn left into the parking lot for the car on the other side of the road to turn right. A hand waved through the windshield.

It took her a second to recognize it was Brad in his civilian vehicle.

With a smile, she pulled in after him and parked.

He was out of his jeep before her and headed over to open her door. "You ready, trouble maker?" His dark eyes were warm.

"For what?"

"Confession. It's good for the soul." There was a flicker of a smile at the corner of his mouth.

Once inside, the waitress soon had them seated with a bowl of warm tortilla chips and salsa.

"So, what have you got for me?" Brad studied her and took a long sip off his coke.

"Well, I think I have the nail for the killer's coffin."

Brad raised an eyebrow, waiting patiently.

"I know who did it. It's not who you think. It wasn't Frank or Sylvia." Elise shoved a chip into her mouth.

Brad nodded with his face devoid of emotion.

"Quit using your detective mind skills on me. I'm saying it wasn't Frank." Elise repeated.

"I heard you the first time. Are you going to tell me why you're saying that?"

"Frank couldn't have done it because at the time of his death he was at the movies, and then like you discovered, calling his parole officer. I knew he couldn't have done it regardless because twenty minutes wasn't enough time for him to get to the dealership and back. I tried it the other day. Barring traffic, I was able to make a round trip without stopping in twenty-five."

The waitress approached with two plates of tacos. Elise's mouth watered at their beautiful sight. Her stomach growled, and she suddenly didn't want to talk anymore.

Brad crunched his taco loudly and seemed to be digesting her hypothesis at the same time. "So, who was it then?"

"Mrs. McMahon."

"Ahh, our doggy kidnapper. Tell me why."

Quickly, she filled him in on her excursion at Crystal's. At the last moment, she left out the part about blackmailing Lavina. She decided to keep it as an ace-in-a-hole just in case she needed it later.

With a deep exhale that flared his nostrils, Brad shook his head. "I have my doubts that it was her. I'm sorry to say this, but you're too close to the case."

"What? Didn't you hear everything I said?"

"Yeah I did. And I've already been over that scenario."

"Don't you remember how the dog acted?"

"I did. I think they got rid of him because Herman hated Mrs. McMahon due to the fact that she was cheating on Cameron with Eric. After his death, she didn't want the dog around incase his aggression threw suspicion on her. You need to consider the fact that she drove two hours away to give Herman to an animal rescue that specializes in adopting dogs, rather than putting him down. That doesn't sound like someone who'd poison their husband and let him get smashed by a train. Or let anyone else do it, for that matter."

"You don't know women. We are capable of anything. And, you're the one who said the killer was someone close to him."

"Actually, I said Cameron knew the killer. Which is why you don't see what's right before your eyes."

Elise looked warily over at him.

"I got a phone call on my way here. I was told they're putting together an arrest warrant for your friend, Lavina."

"What?" Elise choked on a piece of lettuce and grabbed for her drink. When she was done, her hands were shaking. "Don't let them do this, Brad. They're wrong. Please, don't let it happen."

Brad's mouth dipped in sadness. He sighed and ran his hands through his short hair. "Look. I know this is hard. I get it. But they have video evidence showing that she was there on that day."

Elise rubbed her temples. "How can you prove it was her?"

"You know that dark figure? The one we couldn't identify? Well, the camera from the convenience store caught a white convertible pulling up, and the figure from the video got out of it. That car is registered to Lavina. And, there is a shot of her face before she slid the glasses and hat on. It was her, Elise. She was there."

"What about innocent until proven guilty?"

"Absolutely. But our job is to gather enough evidence to prove that a suspect is guilty. And, I checked back with the receptionist at Friendly Smiles Dentistry, and she insists it was a female who rescheduled the appointment."

"That still could have been Sylvia or even Mrs. McMahon."

"I don't know if you knew this, but Lavina also was being extorted."

Elise nearly cried as her ace flushed down the hole. "By Eric!" She caught the look in his eye and bit her lip.

Brad frowned. "So, you did know that. Why didn't you tell me earlier?"

"And help you build a case against an innocent person? By the way, since the extortionist was Eric, that should make you take a closer look at him."

"Except, with Cameron dead, Lavina inherits his estate. And with that kind of money she could buy protection to make sure Eric stayed quiet. Permanently."

She pushed the plate of tacos away from her. "I feel sick. I can't believe this is happening."

"I'm sorry, Elise. The powers above me made the decision. They were really pushing for an arrest before this week's reading of the will. By state law, if a recipient of a will is accused of the murder of that person, they no longer stand to inherit anything. I guess the Captain thought this would make things much easier in the long run."

"So, it's a nice, tidy case for the executor since it gets rid of the inheriting child." She couldn't help the bitter tone.

"I didn't mean to make it sound like that. She'll need your support more now than ever."

"This is bull crap, Brad." She had more to say to him, but something niggled at her about their earlier conversation. She couldn't concentrate on it now. Instead, she gave him a stiff smile, purposely showing how angry she was, and threw down a twenty dollar bill. Then, gathering up her stuff, she headed out to her car.

❊ ❊ ❊

A short while later she was driving up the side of Mt. Treacle, keeping a sharp eye out for any white crosses. The road twisted up in tight curves with a narrow shoulder that accentuated the steep cliff on one side, and a sheer bank rising upwards on the other. She shivered, imagining how devastating it would be to lose the ability to brake on this road.

There! She saw a white blur as she passed.

Elise slowed around the bend and finally found a place to pull off. Cautiously, she walked back on the nearly nonexistent shoulder, hoping there wouldn't come a car flying around the bend to smash her over the bluff.

As she approached the white cross, she looked over the railing at the scene of the old accident.

Spread out below in reds and blues and yellows, like a grandmother's nine-patch quilt, was a bed of flowers.

Delphinium.

Just like that, she knew who killed Cameron.

And the killer was about to strike again.

29

The wind whipped her dark hair in her face. She ducked behind the guard rail and twisted it tightly against her scalp. Palming her phone, she pulled up her list of contacts and stabbed Brad's name.

The connection wheel spun without ringing. No service.

For a second she wanted to give up and run back to town so someone else could handle this. Let someone else lead the rescue.

Something she'd always done in the past. Never the leader, always the watcher.

She peeked down into the gully. There was no time to watch now.

As silently as she could, she climbed over the guard rail and crouched among the brush on the other side. There was a thin trail among the undergrowth that led steeply down the embankment. Her hand gripped the base of a bush for support as her foot slid looking for stability. She reached for the next scrub, and the next, slowly skating her way to the bottom. Once there, she ducked low among the delphinium which had crept right to the edge of the bowl of the basin.

Her pulse pounded in her throat. If she could just sneak around, she would have the advantage of surprise.

"Hello, Elise."

Every hair rose on her neck. Elise slowly stood up with her heart hammering, already knowing what she would see.

A barrel of a gun pointing straight at her.

"You thought you were so clever. Always snooping around asking your silly questions. And here you are now, making things so easy for me."

Elise lifted her gaze from the end of the barrel to the face behind it.

"Estelle."

"Let me see your hands."

Over Estelle's shoulder, Elise could see a crying Sylvia bound and gagged sitting among the flowers.

"What are you doing?" Elise asked as she raised her hands. "Why are you doing this? You could have easily gotten away with this."

"Gotten away with it." Estelle shook her head in mock pity. "Oh, you poor thing. Do you think that's why I did any of this? To 'get away with it'?" She stepped back, motioning with the gun to have Elise move forward. "Careful. Careful," she warned.

Elise walked through the flowers to stand next to Sylvia. Her brain frantically tried to come up with a plan.

"Is this about revenging Mr. Davis? Aren't you his niece?"

Estelle's lips twisted into a sardonic grin. "His niece...."

"You're not his niece?" Elise's tone fell flat at the knowledge.

"Of course, I'm not his niece. I met him at the Wellness Center. I was his nurse."

"You fell in love."

"I fell in love." Estelle's face softened as her voice trailed away. A wistful expression flitted around her eyes as she gazed out at the horizon. She looked back at Elise sharply. "But, he was too damaged. The loss of his son ruined the best man that ever existed. So, you can see, I wasn't about to let Cameron enjoy his new son. And I can't allow his son to inherit a good life now." She motioned again. "Sit down. Keep your hands in the air."

Elise awkwardly got to her knees next to Sylvia. The pregnant woman had mascara dripping down her face from her tears. She moaned around the sodden gag in her mouth.

"Hang in there. You're going to be okay," Elise whispered.

"Okay?" Estelle laughed. "That's one way to look at it, I suppose. Or dead. I prefer dead."

"How did you get Cameron in the car?" Elise needed to keep her talking. Talking was time.

"That was the easiest part of all. He was always about a hook up. After a few Facebook messages and some half-nude photos, he was raring to meet me for a little tête-à-tête."

"How'd you knock him out?"

"A little poetic justice. Did you know if you ingest delphinium you will suffer from seizures, and eventually death?" She looked out again at the flowers being tussled by the breeze.

"You got him to eat flowers?" Maybe not the wisest way to word it, but Elise was desperate to keep her talking. She could feel time was running out.

"Oh, you're feeling funny, aren't you? No. Although that would have been the perfect ending, it was too impractical. Instead, I had to use something I'd swiped from the clinic. A heavy barbiturate that was a part of Mr. Davis's treatment for his insomnia. Poor man still suffers terrors every night stemming from the accident."

Estelle's gaze darted over to Sylvia sniffling behind her gag. "You know, it made Cameron quite talkative and cooperative those first few minutes. He was quite happy about having a son. Quite giggly about everything really, until the full dose hit. Then...." Estelle drew her thumb across her neck.

"So, why did you write the suicide note then? Uncovering Lavina as his daughter?" Elise purposely tried to make her body appear limp, even as her toe wormed into the ground searching for leverage.

Estelle frowned and flushed slightly with either anger or frustration. "By exposing her, Lavina became a suspect. A rare opportunity really, knowing one of Cameron's kids would be jailed for his death—either his daughter or his son within the womb. I couldn't have planned it better if I tried."

"You were the one who canceled Sylvia's dental appointment."

She grinned. "I was. After scheduling an emergency one for Mr. Davis, it just seemed timely that Sylvia have the one right before it. It was perfect serendipity." She shook her head. "But the police didn't follow either lead like they should have. So here we are. Let's call this Plan B, shall we?" Her finger tapped gently against the trigger in warning.

"Sylvia, how did you feel when you saw all your stuff sitting in the middle of your lawn?" Elise asked. "What did you want to do to Frank?"

"Leave her alone. You want her to be first?" Estelle's eyes narrowed. She raised the gun.

"You ready to see something sweet?" Elise licked her lips. She had just managed to wiggle one foot under her.

"Mmmfff." Sylvia muffled out, capturing Estelle's attention for a millisecond.

That moment was all Elise needed. She sprung upward, her other leg already swinging forward in a kick.

In the same instant, Sylvia launched herself headfirst at Estelle. Estelle instinctively leaped back. But not out of range of Elise's foot landing on the side of her knee. Without a pause, Elise's right forearm came under the hand holding the gun, while her left fist dove into Estelle's throat.

Estelle's scream was silenced into a gurgle. Elise pounced on top of her and flipped her over onto her stomach. She wrenched the gun away and flung it as far as she could.

Sylvia inched over and half lay across Estelle's back. Quickly, Elise untied her gag and arms. As soon as her arms were free, Sylvia grabbed the back of Estelle's hair and pounded her face into the dirt. "You sick, sick woman!"

"Sylvia! Calm down! For the baby's sake! You have to calm down. It's okay. You're okay."

The pregnant woman broke down in tears but finally released Estelle's hair. She looked at her hands as if shocked at what they'd just done. Blinking back tears, she stared at Elise. "What are we going to do now?"

"We'll figure out how to tie her up. I can stay with her while you get to my car."

"Her car is over there." Sylvia pointed to a dirt trail about a hundred feet away.

"Baby? Baby, you okay?"

Startled, both women looked up at the top of the embankment at the sound of a man yelling.

"Frank?"

Frank came sliding down the hill in a cloud of dust. Sylvia pushed herself up. Tears sprung to her eyes as she staggered toward him. "Frank!"

"Oh, baby!" They stumbled into each other's arms and held each other as tight as two people could. When they separated, he bent down and ran his hand along her belly. "Is he okay?"

"He's fine, honey. We're fine. What are you doing here?"

He looked around still dazed. "Painting those darn crosses. I heard voices…." His voice trailed away. Spotting Elise, he yelled, "You okay?"

"Could use a little help here."

Frank hurried over and quickly tied Estelle up using Sylvia's old bonds. "I called the police. They should be here soon."

"How? I didn't have any service?"

"CB radio in my truck. I'm old school, I guess." He took Sylvia's face in his hands and kissed her. "Baby, my life flashed before my eyes seeing you down there. I don't care, I don't care anymore. We've both made mistakes. You're the best thing that's ever happened to me and I can't lose you. We've got to work this out. Life is too short. I know we can fix this."

She kissed him back before wiping under her eyes. "I've barely been able to breathe knowing what I screwed up. I'm so sorry. I'll do whatever it takes, honey." They hugged again and their words dissolved into quiet murmurs. Finally, pulling away, Sylvia turned back to Elise, "You were right. That really was sweet."

30

Three days later, Elise panted hard as she entered her driveway. Her heart thumped inside her chest and her lungs were on fire, but she felt strong. Pulling up her sleeve, she glanced down at her Fitbit. A laugh erupted from her throat. YES! Three minutes faster than the last run. Her best time yet.

She headed up the porch steps and flopped into one of the wicker chairs. Her long legs stretched out in front of her feeling a mixture of both rubbery and powerful. She checked the time again and smiled. Never did she think she could do it, but here she was. Making her dreams come true.

And a confirmation in her email for the completed registration for the half-marathon proved it.

But, as usual, she was late. With a groan, she jumped back to her feet and stumbled into the house. Max gave his welcome meow from on top of the china cabinet.

"Get down from there."

He yawned in response.

Too tired to care, Elise walked into her room, quickly chose a sundress off the hanger and hit the shower. Lavina was coming to pick her up in thirty minutes, and it was time to celebrate.

Out of the shower, she slipped into her sundress and dragged a comb through her wet hair.

A car turned into the driveway. Elise walked to the window to peek out. Not Lavina, but Brad's black jeep.

She hurried outside to meet him. "Hey there."

"How's my favorite trouble maker?" His gaze took in her tan legs under the dress, and he smiled appreciatively.

"It's a good day. On my run this morning I finally figured out why there were twenty-nine vases."

"Oh yeah? Let's hear it."

"That's how old Mr. Davis's son would have been this year. And the flowers were for where he died."

"You really are a detective." Brad grinned, as he reached into his pocket to pull something out. It stuck for a second, and he frowned as he tried to extricate it.

"What's that?" she asked.

"I have something for you."

A squeal of tires heralded Lavina's Camaro racing around the corner. They both turned to watch, one in disbelief and the other with a wry grin.

Lavina pulled in next to Brad with her blue silk scarf blowing and one hand in the air waving like a princess in a parade. "Halloo. The party can start now."

Brad just shook his head. "No seatbelt? Speeding? That was like five driving violations right there."

"Will I always be under your radar?" Lavina batted her eyes at him.

Color rose in his cheeks. "Not on my radar. No, not anymore."

"So, what are you doing here?" Lavina asked before turning to Elise. "Is he invited to our girl's night out?"

"He said he has something for me." Elise pointed. "You know I'm all about the gifts."

"Well, he better have a pretty impressive goody." Lavina sniffed. "You practically accomplished the whole Angel Lake Police Department's job for them. And saved my butt. So, let's see it, Brad."

Brad's smile fell as he caught sight of Elise's left hand. A diamond sparkled on her ring finger.

She caught him staring and rubbed at it subconsciously. "Yeah. Mark and I talked last night. He sent a package a week ago, and I only just now looked at it. Our old wedding album. We're going to maybe... maybe try to give it one more go. I mean, if Sylvia and Frank can do it." She half-heartedly grinned.

Brad winced and swallowed hard. "That's great." He shifted uneasily on his feet.

"I know. It's weird. But, my parents were so heart broken when they found out I was divorcing Mark. His parent's too. He says he's changed. I feel like I owe it to everyone to try it one more time."

"What about you? What do you owe yourself?" His eyes searched hers demanding an answer.

Sadness twisted her core. "We were married ten years, Brad."

He nodded. "Yeah, okay. You have to do what you have to do. I just care about you. I don't want you to get hurt again."

Lavina sighed. "Well, I feel the same way, compadre. What is our girl thinking, I just do not know? And to leave Angel Lake and move back to that unrefined state."

Elise turned between them, trying to lighten the mood. "Just look at your faces! I feel like I'm leaving a couple puppies at the pound. I'll be back for a visit. I promise. Anyway, you still have Mr. G to comfort you."

Lavina smiled and looked at her nails.

"You ever plan on telling me who he is?" Elise asked.

Brad cleared his voice. "Who are you talking about? Lavina's boyfriend?"

Elise arched an eyebrow in his direction. "Oh, you better not know, and keep me still in the dark."

"I don't know, but I have my suspicions."

Lavina smoothly laughed before putting one manicured nail over her lips. "I'll never tell."

"Brad! You know! I can tell you know! And you're just going to tease me with that secret forever, aren't you?" Elise reached over to grab his arm but froze halfway there. She let it drop.

Brad watched the movement with a sad smile. "Secret's safe with me. Anyway, I just came by to see how you were doing."

"What? Did you come all the way here just for that? Wasn't there anything else?" Elise watched him earnestly, her cheeks still feeling flushed from her morning jog.

He looked down at his hand and seemed to remember. "Oh yeah, I wanted to give you these. We. A gift from the police department as a thank you. Maybe you and Lavina can go." He handed over two tickets.

Elise took the tickets and read the name. "The Lion King? Lavina, it's for next weekend. How fun! Tell them all thank you for me!"

Lavina made appropriate noises, but her eyes were soft with sympathy as she contemplated Brad. "Well, it was nice seeing you again, Brad. Elise, darlin', I'll wait for you in the house. I have to use the little girl's room," Lavina sauntered indoors with hips swinging.

Brad glanced at Elise again, and his mouth moved like he wanted to say something more. He cleared his throat and ran his hand along the back of his neck. "Yeah, that was it. Anyway, I've got to get going. I'm helping the church set up their rummage sale and barbecue."

Elise didn't want him to go. "Need extra hands?"

He backed away at her offer and shook his head. "No. Not this time. Sounds like I'll be crawling around in someone's basement pulling out some unwanted crap to sell."

"Okay. Take care then, Brad." As he walked away, she was surprised by the sharp pain in her heart.

He half-heartedly raised his hand before slamming the car door. He backed out onto the road and beeped his horn as he drove away.

Elise watched him go. As she turned back to the house she paused and took a long look.

Just a single story, with wide, chunky shutters and a fat porch that stuck out like the front of a boot. This was the place where she'd finally grown into her own.

She was going to miss this.

With a sigh, she shut the screen door softly behind her. Max immediately hopped down from the buffet to curl around her ankles.

"Come here, boo," she whispered and scooped up the orange fuzz ball. "You aren't going anywhere. Mark's just going to have to learn to like cats." Cuddling him close, she wandered into the kitchen.

Her phone buzzed on the counter. She glanced at it a second, and her eyebrow flickered at the sight of Mark's picture on the screen. Ignoring the call, she kissed the cat on the head and carried him over to the window seat.

On the right side of the picture window hung a painting. Mrs. Campbell had insisted Elise take it the last time she was there.

Nearly all of the canvas was a serene blue. A painting of her own precious Angel Lake.

Her home.

Elise slumped into the seat and buried her face in the cat's fur. What was she doing?

Max purred deeply in her lap, his eyes closing to tiny slits. She stroked around his ears and he rubbed his cheek against her fingers. She thought about who she was when she'd only had herself to rely on.

She knew what she needed to do.

Like a switch flipping, she stood up feeling the sadness drop away. She hurried into the kitchen and reached for the phone to dial Mark.

He answered on the first ring. "Where were you? I'm just about ready to head your way."

"Mark, I have to tell you something. I've grown and changed a lot since I've been back at Angel Lake. I like who I've become."

He exhaled deeply into the phone, sounding impatient. "Elise, I don't have time for this. If I don't get moving now I'll hit rush hour."

"You don't need to worry about traffic. You need to listen. I have a cat now. I run. I was even my own hero when no one else could be." Each sentence made her feel stronger. "I'm not the same woman I was when I left." She thought about it a second longer. "Or maybe I am. Maybe, I've finally climbed out of the box where I've kept myself trapped my whole life trying to please everyone else."

"Elise, Are you drunk? What's with the philosophical speech?"

"I'm telling you it's already too late."

"Elise? Our parents? My job...?"

"Sign the divorce papers, Mark. Go find Stephanie. It's time for the both of us to move on."

She hung up with a satisfied smile, cutting off the cuss words and threats on the other end. She stood and stretched, finally feeling free.

"Darlin'," Lavina yelled from the bathroom. "I always knew underneath the wallflower and cat lady exterior was a woman of steel. I'm just so darn proud of you!" She popped her head out, curls blazing. "Now, you haven't forgotten about our cruise coming up next month, have you? Because I can feel it in my bones that we're going to have quite the adventure."

Made in the USA
Middletown, DE
14 December 2019

80750912R00137